Lucasta

Lucasta

Melinda Hammond

ROBERT HALE · LONDON

© Melinda Hammond 2008
First published in Great Britain 2008

ISBN 978-0-7090-8685-7

Robert Hale Limited
Clerkenwell House
Clerkenwell Green
London EC1R 0HT

www.halebooks.com

2 4 6 8 10 9 7 5 3 1

Typeset in 11¼/15½pt New Century Schoolbook
by Derek Doyle & Associates, Shaw Heath
Printed and bound in Great Britain
by Biddles Limited, King's Lynn

CHAPTER ONE

The small panelled parlour was not the grandest of the reception rooms at Oaklands but during the cold winter months when the icy winds buffeted the ancient house it was by far the warmest. The family had grown accustomed to gathering there before dinner for with a cheerful fire blazing in the hearth the room was very comfortable, unlike the great hall where it was necessary to pull one's chair almost inside the great fireplace to keep warm. It was therefore possible for members of the family to amuse themselves with their various occupations in relative comfort.

Sir Oswald, as befitted the master of the house, was in the best armchair beside the fireplace, one leg resting on a small footstool. He was engaged in studying the newspaper, delivered that day from London. His lady was sitting at a small table with her younger daughter, poring over the fashions described in recent copies of the *Lady's Magazine* while Miss Symonds was more prosaically employed mending a torn sheet.

'This sounds very pretty, Mama.' Camilla pointed to one of the paragraphs on the page. 'It says that the new silks with flowered stripes are all the rage now.'

Sir Oswald looked up from his newspaper.

'And they cost a pretty penny, too.'

Camilla flew across the room to him.

'But you would not see me go to Town in rags, would you, Papa?' She perched on his knee, pouting prettily.

'Baggage,' he chuckled. 'You know I can deny you nothing, my love.'

'My cream tabby silk is packed away upstairs, Mama,' said Miss Symonds. 'Perhaps that could be altered to fit.' She observed Camilla's mouth turn down in disapproval and added, 'It was never worn, Camilla. You need not fear anyone will think you are wearing a reworked gown. I am merely trying to think of the cost.'

'I am glad someone is,' retorted Sir Oswald, retreating once again behind his paper.

Camilla went back to the table.

'I would rather not wear last year's silks, Mama.'

'And nor shall you,' replied Lady Symonds, patting her hand. 'With the gowns you have already, and your new silver muslin, you will look well enough in Town, and once we are there we shall be able to visit the silk mercers and see for ourselves just what will suit you. That is why I am eager to get to Town now, to give us a few weeks to buy you all the clothes you will need for the beginning of the Season. . . .'

Lucasta Symonds looked at her mama and her sister, their heads once more bent over the pages of the magazine and with a sigh she returned to her stitching. She knew how costly it would be for Camilla's first season in Town – heaven knows her father had told her often enough how much had been wasted last year when her own come-out had been curtailed. Lucasta had been unfortunate enough to contract chicken pox at the beginning of the Season and had returned to Oaklands with a trunkful of gowns, gloves, slippers and fans all unused. Her father had railed against the expense and since she had found herself crippled by shyness when presented to a room full of strangers, every one of them sizing her up like a piece of horseflesh, Lucasta had begged him to let her stay at home rather than to repeat the ordeal in the Little Season. Her mother had taken some persuading, but she was now reconciled to her elder daughter staying at home while she concentrated on Camilla's come-out which, she assured her spouse, could not be anything other than a resounding success.

Camilla was the Great Hope of the family. She was classically fair, with pale blonde hair that was her dresser's delight, clustering about her head in angelic curls and framing an almost perfect face. With her dainty figure and graceful manners, Camilla was expected to achieve a great match. For her mama this meant a connection with a noble house while Sir Oswald looked forward to an advantageous marriage settlement to alleviate his own precarious financial state. Camilla's ambition was simple: to have all the London beaux at her feet. As the undisputed local beauty, Camilla was used to being adored and courted by every gentleman to come across her path, and she saw no reason why the same should not happen in Town, a view upheld by her fond mama.

'Even the squire says that you are every bit as beautiful as the Gunning sisters,' said Lady Symonds, pulling Camilla down beside her again. 'If they could come from nowhere and marry dukes, just think what a young lady from a good Shropshire family might achieve.'

'Mama, the Gunning sisters were in their prime nearly thirty years ago,' put in Lucasta, smiling. 'Times have changed somewhat since then.'

'Oh hold your tongue, girl, of course they have not. A pretty girl will always captivate a gentleman, if she is clever enough.'

Camilla smiled.

'And I am very clever, am I not, Mama?'

'You are indeed, my love.'

'So you see, Lucasta, I shall be looking pretty high for a husband. Oh I do wish you could be there to see my success.'

Sir Oswald folded up his paper, saying, 'Now, now, you know it is agreed that Lucasta shall stay at Oaklands and keep house for me.'

'Well, with a houseful of staff I do not think that you can really need her,' said his lady thoughtfully. 'She might be very useful in Town, running errands for me.'

'I assure you I am content to stay at Oaklands,' put in Lucasta. 'I think you would find me very much in the way in Town.'

'Indeed you would,' agreed her fond papa. 'She is staying here and that's an end to it.' He broke off, listening to the sound of voices approaching from the great hall. 'Ah, Ned's here.'

The door burst open and a gentleman strode in, bringing a blast of cold air with him. He was not above average height and of stocky build with a round, good-natured face and an abundance of fair curls imperfectly confined with a ribbon at the nape of his neck. He was dressed in a country-style frock coat, buckskins and muddied top boots which caused a look of disapproval to flicker across Lady Symonds's countenance but this disappeared when she saw who had followed him into the room.

'I found Kennington on the road,' announced Ned cheerfully.

The second gentleman stepped forward to make his bow.

'That sounds as if I was destitute at the roadside,' he said, smiling. 'In fact I am visiting my cousins at Harley. Your servant, Sir Oswald, Lady Symonds. I had planned to call upon you later in the week, but—'

'I told him I am going back to Kent tomorrow and that he had best come home now and take pot luck with us,' Ned interrupted him.

Lucasta paused in her sewing to study the visitor. She recognized his voice, even though it was a little deeper now, and she remembered a long-limbed schoolboy visiting Oaklands when she was a child, but she doubted she would have recognized Viscount Kennington without an introduction. The gangly youth had matured into a tall, elegant gentleman who needed no padding to fill out the broad shoulders of his superfine coat and his tight-fitting buckskins revealed strong, shapely limbs that proclaimed the sportsman. His rich brown hair, that Lucasta remembered flopping untidily over his brow, was neatly confined by a black ribbon and from the fall of frothy lace at his throat to his gleaming top boots he was every inch a fashionable gentleman.

'And we are very glad to have you here,' said Lady Symonds, going across the room to greet her guest. 'My dear Lord Kennington! Why, we have not seen you for . . . oh it must be ten years at least.'

The viscount gave her a singularly sweet smile. That much about him hadn't changed, thought Lucasta with approval. He had been a good-natured youth, always ready to laugh even at himself. She watched him bow gracefully over her mama's hand.

'Once my uncle's health began to fail my visits became very infrequent,' he said. 'But, of course, I saw Ned at Oxford and kept in touch with him.'

Lady Symonds beamed at him and nodded, saying, 'Perhaps you do not remember my daughters.'

From her shadowed corner Lucasta waited to observe

Lord Kennington's reaction. He did not disappoint her. She did not leave her seat, merely inclined her head to him. His bow was perfectly executed and he gave her a friendly smile, but when Camilla came forward make her curtsey there was no disguising the frank admiration in his gaze. He was too much the gentleman to gape, but his grey eyes widened with interest and his smile deepened into something much more charming. Lucasta was not surprised: she had seen too many gentlemen react thus when they were first introduced to her sister. It did not worry her that the gentlemen did not give her a second glance if Camilla was in the room: after all, she was well aware that straight brown hair and brown eyes, however, dark, could not compare with Camilla's golden curls and blue eyes. She watched now as Lord Kennington bowed over Camilla's hand.

'But of course I remember you,' he was saying to her, 'you sometimes joined us when we played cricket.'

Ned gave a crack of laughter.

'No, no, Adam, that was Lucasta.'

'Heavens yes, I remember,' cried Camilla. 'You called her Luke, until Mama forbade it, saying it was most improper.'

'But much less of a mouthful,' murmured Lucasta.

'It is a beautiful name,' replied Lady Symonds, adding with a sigh, 'I was much addicted to poetry when I was younger.'

Ned chuckled as he poured a glass of wine for his guest.

'Aye, but she should have been a boy. Camilla now, she never played ball-games: always afraid of getting grass stains on her petticoats.'

'And quite right too,' murmured the viscount, raising his glass to Camilla as he treated her to another of his charming smiles.

Camilla blushed, looked away then peeped back under her

lashes, her cherry-lips curving into a shy smile. From her corner Lucasta observed the viscount's reaction: he was captivated.

'Well, well,' cried Sir Oswald in jovial tones. 'So you will stay to dine with us, my lord. Lucasta, go and tell Piggott to lay another cover. Pray sit down, my lord, then we may all be comfortable!'

Lucasta did not consider the evening remotely comfortable. With her come-out looming, Camilla was delighted to practise flirting with a real viscount and Lucasta was dismayed to watch her parents actively encouraging her. She realized that this was inevitable: Viscount Kennington was unmarried and in possession of a substantial fortune in his own right, as well as being heir to an earldom and extensive estates. He was just the sort of eligible suitor they wanted for Camilla and they proceeded to go out of their way to attach him. Sir Oswald was abnormally hearty and his lady so gushing that Lucasta was faintly embarrassed. Only Ned behaved normally, treating the viscount with his usual bluff good-humour and Lucasta reflected that if it had not been for her brother's occasional remarks, she would have spent the whole evening saying nothing at all.

Lord Kennington did not appear in the least put out by the attentions of his hosts and responded with polite good-humour. When Camilla asked him with studied innocence if he would be attending the assembly in Shrewsbury the following evening there was a decided gleam in his eye when he said he would not dream of missing it. Lucasta was not surprised, therefore, when the next day saw another flurry of activity as Camilla's trunks were unpacked again.

'But, Mama,' Lucasta murmured mischievously, 'I thought you had given up the idea of going to the assembly before setting off for Town.'

'That was before we knew Lord Kennington would be there,' replied Camilla, pulling out another of her gowns.

'Well, I hope he is worth it.' Lucasta looked at the robes and tissue paper scattered around the room. 'There is another two hours' work for Annie to pack all these away again.'

'Well,' retorted Lady Symonds, 'since you say you do not care to come to the assembly with us, you may pack it all tonight while we are out.'

'Certainly! I would much rather be so employed than watching you fawning over Lord Kennington. But who knows, perhaps he will not turn up.'

CHAPTER TWO

Lucasta learned early the following morning that the viscount had indeed attended the assembly. At the breakfast table the talk was all of Lord Kennington.

'I am so pleased I wore my new gown, for it looked very well, did it not, Mama?'

'Indeed, the viscount was quite captivated.' Lady Symonds gave a triumphant smile. 'He danced almost every dance with Camilla, you know. He barely looked at another lady, although, of course, there was no one there to hold a candle to dear Camilla. He was even kind enough to escort us to our carriage when we left.'

Lucasta frowned.

'Is that not showing a little too much partiality, Mama?'

'Pho, a country dance – what does it matter? Better for Camilla to secure his interest before we get to Town, where there will be any number of pretty girls vying for his attention.'

'And what do you think?' cried Camilla, 'He has accepted an offer to go fishing with Papa tomorrow.'

Lucasta turned her attention to her breakfast. She could not like this sudden excess of friendliness, but she suspected that the viscount had grown used to such sycophantic behaviour – indeed, she reflected sourly, he must positively enjoy it.

Once she had the viscount's assurance that he would soon be following them to Town, Lady Symonds returned to her arrangements for their visit to London with renewed vigour and when the ladies gathered for a late breakfast the following day – Sir Oswald having gone off to meet the viscount some hours earlier – she broke off from the recital of her plans for the day only long enough to assure Camilla that they would find time to take a walk down to the river in the afternoon.

'You must wear your villager hat, my love, the one with the blue ribbons that match your eyes, and bring your Paisley shawl: there is always a breeze down by the river and I would not want you to catch a chill. Or perhaps we could unpack your blue redingote.'

'Heavens, Mama, be careful,' murmured Lucasta, buttering a piece of toast. 'Too much elegance will frighten the fish.'

'That is enough, miss,' retorted her mother. 'Such saucy remarks are most unbecoming.'

'But surely Camilla would be better wrapped in her warm cloak than parading beside the river in her finery and looking very out of place.'

'Then you know very little about it,' snapped her sister. 'I am sure Lord Kennington will want to see me looking my best.'

Lucasta's eyes twinkled with mischief.

'If Ned had not been obliged to return to Kent I am sure he would say that having a couple of chattering females nearby was the last thing any fisherman would want!'

Lucasta realized that she would not be required to join in this proposed treat and once she had completed all the household tasks that fell to her lot she decided to spend the rest of the time until the dinner hour in her favourite spot, the tree house.

There had been a tree house in the ancient lime at Oaklands for generations and in times gone by it had been used by the family for summer dinner parties and even, it was rumoured, for gatherings of a far more licentious nature. Sir Oswald, however, had no time for such folly and the children had been allowed to use the tree house as their own special place. The octagonal building rested between the giant branches of the tree. It had windows on all sides except for the panel incorporating the door and gave excellent views over the park. A narrow flight of steps climbed steeply against the massive tree trunk to provide access and the estate's carpenter had undertaken to keep both the steps and the building in good order for the children, off-setting the minor expense incurred against other, more necessary works and thus avoiding the inevitable claim by Sir Oswald that the tree house was a waste of money and should be dismantled.

Lucasta told no one of her plans for the afternoon and since her mama and sister were too preoccupied with their plans to walk to the river they did not think to ask, so she collected her book, slipped out of the house and ran the few hundred yards to the tree house. The furniture had long since been removed, but Lucasta merely wrapped her cloak about her and made herself comfortable upon the floor. With the early spring sunshine pouring in through the windows the little room was surprisingly warm, and she was soon lost in her novel.

It was some hours later when she heard someone climbing up the steps. She was not alarmed, thinking it must be one of the footmen sent to find her, but she could not suppress a little gasp of surprise when Lord Kenington stepped into the room.

'Oh.' He hesitated in the doorway. 'I am sorry, I did not expect anyone to be here.' He gave her a wry smile. 'I remembered the games Ned and I played here and as I was riding past, I could not resist coming up for one last look.'

'Then please, stay and look around, if you wish.'

Lucasta closed her book, but she made no move to get up, merely watching him as he closed the door and came into the room.

'If I remember correctly, the last time I was here it was a pirate ship.'

'Yes,' muttered Lucasta. 'And you refused to let Camilla and me come in.'

He turned to look at her, a smile lurking in his grey eyes.

'We were repelling boarders.'

She laughed at that, and his smile grew.

'I hope you do not still hold that against me, Miss Symonds? I was only a scrubby schoolboy then: I hope I should not be so ungallant to you now.'

'No, I am sure you would not.'

He dropped down to floor, leaning against the wall some distance away, but the curve of the building put him at an angle, and when he stretched his long legs before him, his shining top boots were almost touching her soft kid slippers. It took a conscious effort from Lucasta not to withdraw from him.

'Is this where you come when you want to be alone, Miss Symonds?'

She nodded.

'No one ever uses it now, but Ned is married and lives in Kent with his own young family, so I hope that when they visit us in future years his children may enjoy this place as much as we did.'

'Yes, I remember whenever I came to stay at Harley it was one of the highlights of my visit, to come here with my cousins.' He laughed. 'We played ball games on the lawns and allowed you to be an honorary boy. You see, I *do* remember it, Miss Symonds: my apologies for thinking it was your sister.'

She lifted her hand in a small, dismissive gesture, but she was pleased.

'Had you much sport at the river, my lord?'

'No. The fish were not biting and your father's hip made it uncomfortable for him to sit down for too long, so we gave it up soon after lunch and walked the long way back through the woods – why does that make you smile?'

'No reason, sir. You said you were riding – does that mean you do not stay for dinner?'

'Alas, no. My cousins have invited a few special guests for dinner tonight and I must be there. After that, my visit to Harley is at an end, so this will be my last visit to Oaklands.'

'Well, as Mama takes Camilla to London tomorrow you will have no reason to call.' Lucasta's hands flew to her mouth and she looked at him in horror. 'I am sorry, I should not have said that; I was thinking out loud.'

'No matter. Is it really so obvious?'

Her eyes twinkled back at him.

'Well, yes, it is. Besides, Ned was forever telling us that the fishing at Harley is much superior to our own small stretch of river, so I could not think why you should want to spend the day here if it was not to see Camilla.' She observed his wry smile and took pity on him. 'After all, she *is* stunningly beautiful.'

'A diamond,' he agreed. 'I hope to renew our acquaintance

17

in London. You travel tomorrow, you said?'

'Mama and Camilla only. I shall stay here to look after Papa.'

He raised an eyebrow, but did not comment upon it and a few moments later he jumped to his feet.

'I must get back to Harley and you, I am sure, will want to get on with your book. Good day to you, Miss Symonds. Let us hope it is not another ten years before we meet again.'

With a bow and a smile he was gone. Lucasta listened to the sound of his footsteps on the stairs, then she scrambled up and looked out of the window in time to see him trotting off down the drive. She realized with a little jolt of surprise how easy it had been to talk to him. She had not felt the least shy in his company. He was certainly very taken with Camilla, and it occurred to her that if he was serious enough to make her an offer, Camilla could wish for no better husband than Viscount Kennington.

CHAPTER THREE

On an icy March day Lady Symonds set off for London with Camilla, and Lucasta was left with little to do at Oaklands. With Piggott and his wife to run the house she wondered why her father had been so keen to have her stay with him. He had never sought Lucasta's company and when they did meet at mealtimes he did not speak to her except to criticize or to issue some new instruction. Their first dinner together after Camilla and Lady Symonds's departure was taken in near silence, but Lucasta bore this cheerfully: she was well aware that Camilla had always been his favourite but it seemed that with the imminent prospect of Camilla's marriage, her father wanted to improve his relations with his elder daughter, and she hugged this small hope to her.

At breakfast the following day her father greeted her cheerfully, and her spirits rose even more.

'Well my dear, you must instruct Cook to put on a good dinner for us this evening, for we have a guest. Squire Woodcote is joining us.'

'I see.' She looked up hopefully, 'Does that mean you will be dining alone with him?'

'Indeed it does not, my girl. I shall expect you to play the hostess and to extend every courtesy to our guest.' Lucasta's spirits, riding so high a moment earlier, plummeted. 'You need not look so downcast, madam! Arnold Woodcote is an old friend and you have known him for ever. He is not some stranger that you have never seen, so you cannot tell me you are shy of him!'

Lucasta swallowed her retort. It was true that she had known Squire Woodcote since she was a baby but she could not like him. She disliked his jovial familiarity, the way he would pull her onto his knee and demand a kiss or allow his hand to linger on her arm whenever he came near. With her mother present she had always felt protected but now she, Lucasta, would be playing hostess and she was vaguely uneasy. She delayed going down to the little parlour as long as she could and wore a demure, high-necked gown with long gloves so that she need not feel the squire's hot, flabby fingers on her skin. Even so, she could hardly suppress a shiver when he pressed his mouth to her fingers.

'Ah, Miss Symonds, so your sister has gone off to enjoy herself in London and you are left behind! Well, we must count London's loss our gain, eh?'

Lucasta drew her hand away and tried to smile. The squire was a robust man with iron-grey hair who was happy to boast that he wouldn't see fifty again. His cheeks were reddened by an abundance of fresh air and red wine and his portly figure was due to overindulgence at the dinner-table. He had been a widower for many years, with no children of his own, and to this fact Lady Symonds ascribed his fondness for Lucasta and her sister. When they were children he had never left without pressing a coin into their hands, but the price for this was that he had been allowed to kiss them. Camilla had never minded, but Lucasta would have much preferred him to keep his money and his kisses to himself.

'Well, Symonds, you may say that your little Camilla is a

diamond, but this girl is a pearl,' he declared, leering at Lucasta. 'And you have her all to yourself for the next few months eh?'

'Indeed I do, Arnold,' agreed Sir Oswald. 'We shall be as snug as bugs, will we not, my dear?'

Lucasta could think of no reply to her father's uncharacteristic jollity and was grateful when Piggott came in to announce that dinner awaited them. The food could not be faulted and Mr Woodcote praised every dish. Lucasta was only glad that the long table ensured that she was seated far enough away from the squire that he could not reach out to pat her hand or, even worse, to touch her leg with his foot, something he had done at other family dinners when the wine had been flowing too freely. At the end of the meal she retired to the little parlour with her embroidery, which she only put aside when the tea tray was brought in and she was obliged to serve the gentlemen. As soon as she was able she returned to her needlework and at eleven o'clock she retired to her room, thankful that the gruelling night was over.

She was seated at her dressing table, brushing out her hair when her father came in without ceremony. He dismissed her maid with a curt word, and stood glaring down at his daughter.

'Well, miss, you will know why I am here.'

She looked at him blankly.

'Why, no, sir . . .'

'Damnation girl, I have never been so ashamed of you in all my life! What do you mean, treating my old friend so coldly?' He snatched up her gown which was lying over a chair. 'And how dare you appear in this dowdy rag? Anyone would think you were a Quaker!'

Lucasta shrank back before his rage, but she forced herself to reply.

'I do not like the way the squire looks at me.'

'You'll allow him to look at you all he wants,' raged Sir Oswald. 'And to do a great deal more, if I have my way!'

'Wh-whatever do you mean?'

'I mean that he is minded to wed you!'

'No!' Lucasta shuddered.

'Oh yes! Do you think I want you here, eating me out of house and home for the rest of your life? What with the fortune we wasted on you last year I feel very hardly done by, my girl. It's time you paid your way, and if Woodcote is prepared to be generous then I am happy to see you wed him.'

'Please, Papa—'

'Don't you come mewling and crying to me, Lucasta. You will do as you are told! The squire is coming to dinner again tomorrow night and you will be on hand to receive him, and wearing your best gown, if you please. I want him to know you are a lady, not a nun.'

'No!' Lucasta shot up, quivering with rage. 'You cannot treat me like this!'

Sir Oswald pulled himself up to his full height and stepped towards her, glowering.

'I shall treat you how I like, my girl, and you will do as you are told.' He turned and strode to the door. 'And don't think I will let you plead a headache and keep to your room, because if you do that I shall fetch you downstairs in your petticoats if necessary!'

He slammed out of the room and she was left staring at the closed door. How could he expect her to marry the squire? He was of an age with her father; the very thought of it made her feel sick. She sank down onto her chair again. If only her mother was here! A moment's reflection convinced her that her father had deliberately waited until

Mama was out of the way before announcing his plan. She tried to think calmly. All she had to do was hold out until Mama returned. The thought of sustaining nightly arguments with her father was daunting, and she decided it might be better to write to her mama and explain the situation. As her maid tiptoed back into the room Lucasta gave her a reassuring smile and continued with her preparations for bed. She had only to be firm. After all, she lived in a civilized society: no young lady could be married off against her will.

Lucasta dressed with care the next evening, choosing an open robe of blue satin over a cream quilted petticoat. Her father insisted she came down to the little parlour before Mr Woodcote arrived and he looked her over critically.

'Hmm, you have a good figure,' he muttered, walking around her. He reached out and snatched away the fichu she had arranged around her shoulders. 'No need for that: a man likes to see the goods he is buying.'

Lucasta's face flamed. She wanted to put hands up to her low neckline but she knew it was pointless and would only draw attention to her own discomfort. When the squire arrived she greeted him coldly, suppressing a shudder when he looked greedily at her bosom.

'Perhaps, Sir Oswald, you would allow me the privilege of escorting Miss Symonds into dinner?'

'Of course.'

Sir Oswald stood aside to allow Mr Woodcote to take his place. Lucasta placed her hand upon the squire's sleeve and immediately he pulled her closer. The walk across the great hall to the dining-room had never seemed so long. She forced herself to remain calm and ignored the squire's hints that she should move up to sit beside him so that they might all be cosy. The gentlemen did not talk to her during the dinner, but she felt the squire's eyes constantly upon her, and she could not enjoy her meal. She refused the wine at the table but once she had left the gentlemen to their brandy and made her way back to the panelled parlour, she wondered if this had been wise: she had yet to endure another hour or so of the squire's company. Sitting alone, her courage began to fail her. Remembering her father's threats to drag her from her room, she dared not retire, so she decided to fetch herself a glass of wine to bolster her spirits. She swiftly crossed the great hall and slipped through the servants' passage to the butler's pantry. As she expected, it was empty, for Sir Oswald liked Piggott to remain in attendance in the dining-room while he plied his gentlemen guests with brandy. What she had not expected was that the connecting door between the pantry and the drawing-room should be ajar. She would have to be extremely careful if she was to pour herself a glass of wine from one of the decanters standing open on the side table. Any noise could bring Piggott in to investigate and might even alert her father. She picked up a clean cup from the shelf and moved silently to the side table, making sure she kept well away from the open door. She could hear the gentlemen talking, the chink of glass as more brandy was served. She began to fill her cup, but stopped when she heard her name.

'. . . Lucasta's not cold, Arnold, she's a maid and she's been kept well away from men. You will find her warm enough in your bed, I'll vow.'

'You may well be right, Oswald.' The squire gave a low chuckle that made Lucasta's flesh creep. 'She can't hold a candle to her sister, of course, but I know your good lady has *her* marked out for great things. No, Lucasta is a fine girl, I'll grant you that, and she's strong, I've no doubt she can provide me with a quiverful of brats. Must have an heir, you see, Oswald, the older I get the more I wants someone to look after me in my old age.'

'Well, my daughter will fill that role very well. She's a good housekeeper.'

'Ah. Fine pair of bubbies, too . . . by gad, sir, just thinking of 'em makes me go hot!'

'That's why I thought we should get this matter dealt with as soon as possible. No point in delaying if you are willing, Arnold.'

'Willing? Of course I am willing, man! I procured the special licence, just as you suggested: all we have to do now is persuade that little gel of yours to say yes.'

'Oh she'll agree.' There was a coldness in Sir Oswald's voice that sent a chill running through Lucasta.

'Well, then, old friend, what are we waiting for?'

There was a chink, as if glasses were being touched together.

'I'll get the parson here tomorrow and we'll have you married by dinner time.'

'And bedded, too, just to make sure of the gel,' cackled the squire. 'By gad if I don't feel ready for her now—'

'You'd be well advised not to say anything untoward this evening,' growled Sir Oswald. 'We don't want to scare her off. Tomorrow, a little brandy and laudanum will make her compliant. . . .'

Lucasta leaned against the table, feeling slightly sick. Silently she set the decanter in its place and fled back to the parlour. She drew a chair up to the fire and sat very straight, her hands gripping tightly to the wooden arms. How could they discuss her thus? Anger raged through her. How could they talk about her in such terms, and with Piggott standing in the room. She had always known that her father paid little heed to the servants, but in this matter – it shocked her to realize that he had discussed the marriage of his daughter as coolly as he would have discussed bringing a bull in to service his best heifer. With a sinking heart she realized that her father had planned the whole: he intended to marry her off while her mother was away, knowing that she would object to the match. Fear began to replace her anger. She had failed to catch a husband and her reluctance to try again this season had sealed her fate: her father wanted to recover what he could from a poor investment. It was well known that the squire was a wealthy man; no doubt he would pay handsomely for her. Lucasta shuddered, then squared her shoulders: they would be joining her soon, and not by so much as a look must she show that she knew of their plans. Her choices were limited, but of one thing she was certain: she would not marry Squire Woodcote.

CHAPTER FOUR

A fine drizzle had set in by the time Lord Kennington took his leave of his cousins. Low cloud added to the misty greyness of the March day and he wondered aloud if he should have delayed his journey.

'Since her grace was expectin' you two days since, we needs to crack on,' opined his groom with the familiarity of an old retainer.

'Quiet, Potts. My godmother is not the sort of female to have the vapours because I am a day or two late,' retorted Adam, adding judiciously, 'but perhaps it is as well we do not delay any longer. To hell with this rain, it is turning the lane into a bog!'

Potts did not deign to reply but sat in silence beside his master as he negotiated the muddy lanes without mishap and soon they were bowling south along a well-made highway. The drizzle showed no signs of abating; it dripped from the curricle's waxed hood and puddled in the footwell. There was no traffic on the road, the only sign of life being a solitary cloaked figure, bag in one hand, striding towards them along the grass verge.

'Poor lad,' grunted Potts. 'This ain't a day to be walkin' anywhere.'

Adam was about to agree with him when the figure became aware of the approaching carriage and looked up. Adam found himself staring into the startled face of Miss Lucasta Symonds.

Immediately he brought his team to a stand.

'Miss Symonds! Whatever brings you so far from home in this weather?'

She put down her portmanteau and regarded him nervously.

''It is not a matter that need concern you, my lord. Please, drive on.'

It had been instinct and good manners that had caused the viscount to stop, but now it took a conscious effort for him to ignore the voice in his head advising him to do as she requested. If it had been the enchanting Camilla on the road he would not even have considered leaving her, but there was nothing enchanting about the bedraggled figure at the roadside. The tendrils of hair that had escaped from her boyish cap were curled wetly around her face, and her brown eyes held a distinctly guilty look. He observed her leather boots and guessed that beneath the long cloak wrapped tightly around her body she would be wearing breeches. His curiosity was aroused. He handed the reins to his groom, murmuring, 'Not a word of this to anyone, Potts.'

'It's a good job you mentioned that, me lord, me bein' in the habit of discussing your affairs over a glass o' Dutch gin!'

But the viscount had already jumped down from the curricle.

'Do not be alarmed, ma'am, I mean you no harm.'

'Then I pray you will leave me alone.'

'Dash it all, Miss Symonds, you are alone on a public highway, dressed as a boy – I cannot drive on!'

'But it is nothing to do with you,' she said, a touch of

desperation in her voice.

He smiled at her.

'Tell me.'

'I – um – I am walking to Shrewsbury.'

'Shrewsbury! But that is all of ten miles from here.'

'Yes, but I can catch the direct mail to London from there. I am going to Kent, you see, to – to stay with my brother Ned.' He raised his brows and she hurried on, 'I – um, thought it best to dress like this since I am t-travelling alone.'

'You are running away.'

'No!' Reading the disbelief in his countenance she dropped her gaze. 'Well, yes.'

'Miss Symonds,' he said gently, 'this cannot be wise.'

She wrung her hands together.

'It is necessary. Now, will you not drive on, and forget that you have seen me?'

'No, I am afraid I cannot do that. It would not be right to leave you here unprotected. What time is your coach?'

'I do not know.'

'And where in Shrewsbury does it stop?'

'I am not quite sure . . .'

'It seems to me, Miss Symonds, that you are not very well prepared.'

'This is not something I have been planning, sir! But it – it became clear to me that I had to get away.'

He looked up and down the deserted highway.

'We should not stand here getting wet. Let me help you up into my carriage: you may shelter there while you tell me what has happened to make you fly from your home. You need not be afraid,' he added, seeing her wary look. 'My horses can stand a little longer, and we shall leave your portmanteau where it is, so that you can climb down and walk away from me whenever you wish.'

She subjected him to a prolonged gaze which he returned with a smile and at last she nodded.

'Very well, my lord.'

'Good. Potts, you will go to the horses' heads.'

'Yes my lord.'

'Oh but I would not turn your groom out—'

'You need not worry about Potts, he is used to being out in all weathers and you will note that he is wearing an oiled coat.' He handed her into the curricle and climbed up beside her. 'And talking of coats, where did you find your boots and breeches?'

'They were Ned's once, and had been kept in the dressing-up box we used when we played at charades.' She paused while he spread a thick rug over her knees. 'Thank you, my lord. It is much better in here, out of the rain.'

'I am glad you think so. Now, Miss Symonds, explain yourself.'

She did not look at him, and sat for a moment clasping and unclasping her hands in her lap. He waited patiently.

'If – if I had stayed at the house today I should have been forced into a distasteful marriage.'

'Dear me.'

She looked up at him, reproach in her brown eyes.

'You think I am hysterical, perhaps, but to be forced, against one's will—'

'My dear Miss Symonds surely no one would do such a thing.'

He heard a sob and glanced down at the figure beside him. She was hunting in her pockets for a handkerchief. He said nothing and after a few moments when she had blown her nose and wiped her eyes she took a breath and began to talk again.

'M-my father is determined to see me wed. He spent a great deal of money last year for my presentation but I contracted the chicken pox and everything had to be cancelled.'

'That must have been very disappointing.'

To his surprise she shook her head.

'I loathed the short time I spent in London. They call it the marriage mart, but to me it felt more like a cattle mart, where one is inspected and looked over like so much meat for sale . . .' she gulped. 'And, and I do not find it easy to converse with strangers.'

'But you are talking quite easily to me,' he pointed out.

'But you are not a stranger. You are Ned's friend.'

'Of course.' He said solemnly, 'And we played cricket together.'

His sally was rewarded with a watery chuckle. The horses stamped impatiently.

'So your papa is eager for you to marry. That is not so unusual, in fact it is only natural that he should wish to see you settled.'

'He wants to sell me off,' she said bitterly. 'Last night I overheard him talking with Squire Woodcote. They have devised a plan to marry me off while Mama is in London.' She took another shuddering breath, keeping her head bowed. Adam had to strain to hear her words. 'The s-squire had a special licence, and Papa said he would summon Parson Maebury today to perform the ceremony. He w-was going to force me to marry Squire Woodcote.'

The viscount shook his head.

'He can do nothing of the sort. You only have to tell the parson that you do not wish to go through with it.'

Her disconcertingly straight gaze was turned to him once more.

'That may not be possible, if one has been forced to drink brandy, or dosed with laudanum.'

'Good God! I cannot credit it.'

'Can you not? I assure you I should not have embarked upon this desperate course if I did not believe my father would carry out his threat.'

Adam frowned.

'I have met the squire,' he said at last. 'Why, he is old enough to be your father.'

'It is not only that: if he was kind, then I might be persuaded, but I have seen the way he looks at me, and I c-cannot bear to think of him touching me. . . .'

She shuddered. Adam felt a chill run down his own spine. She stirred beside him.

'I should go now, if I am to reach Shrewsbury before night-fall.'

'No. I have a suggestion, Miss Symonds. You said that your father wished to conclude this marriage while Lady Symonds is in London. Am I to understand your mama would not like this match?'

'I am sure she would not want me to be forced into a marriage, my lord.'

'Very well then. I am on my way to visit my godmother. Let me take you to her – I have lost a little time but we should still be able to accomplish the journey today. From there I will take you on to London, to Lady Symonds. I shall ask my godmother to allow one of her female servants to accompany you. What do you say to that?'

She gazed up at him, misty-eyed.

'You would do that for me?'

'I am actually doing very little, since I am going on to Town anyway.'

'Then, yes, thank you, sir, I will accept your kind offer.'

'Good.' He picked up the reins. 'Potts, secure the lady's bag, if you please!'

Tight-lipped with disapproval, the groom collected the portmanteau, stowed it safely away then nimbly jumped up behind the curricle as it moved off. Adam wondered if it was having to sit out in the rain that was causing his groom to scowl, or his decision to help a young lady run away from home. Either way he would make a grim travelling companion. Adam glanced at the stiff little figure beside him and thought wryly that his new passenger did not look to be much happier.

'Shall you be pursued, do you think?' he asked, to break the uneasy silence.

Miss Symonds gave this some thought.

'I do not think so. My father never leaves his room before noon, and it cannot be much more than that now.'

Lord Kennington took out his pocket watch.

'It wants but twenty minutes to one o'clock, Miss Symonds.'

'Then I doubt that he has yet realized I am missing. Where does your godmother live?'

'Worcestershire. She has a pretty little house near Hansford, a few miles south from Bromsgrove.'

Miss Symonds nodded sagely.

'You travel by Bridgnorth and Kidderminster?'

'I do indeed, ma'am, well done.'

She managed a faint smile.

'It is not so very surprising. There are some very good maps at Oaklands, and I like to study them, and dream that one day I might travel a little.'

'Well dream no more, Miss Symonds, because today you will surely be travelling no small distance! I hope you enjoyed a good breakfast: for we will not be not stopping to eat if we wish to reach Hansford before dark.'

Lucasta reached into her jacket pocket and brought out a rather flattened packet.

'I took the precaution of bringing some of Cook's raised pie with me. Would you like a little, my lord?'

She had already removed her gloves and began to break up the pie with her fingers.

Lord Kennington laughed and held out his hand.

'I do not mind if I do, Miss Symonds!'

CHAPTER FIVE

Despite the continuing rain they made good time to Bridgnorth, but the road from there to Kidderminster was in a poor state, and the viscount was obliged to rein in his team. However, matters improved after Kidderminster, when a good road and fresh horses allowed the viscount to make up some of the lost time. Lucasta cast a glance at the matched bays now harnessed to the curricle. 'These are not hired horses, I think?'

'No. I sent them ahead of me when I knew I was travelling into Worcestershire.'

'And no doubt you sent your man ahead of you to Coombe Chase with the baggage wagon.'

'I did.' He heard the laughter in her voice and added coldly, 'What is there in that to amuse you, Miss Symonds?'

'Why, nothing. Merely that Camilla would be very cross if she knew of the high treat I am enjoying. She and Mama travelled post, you see, and Mama's letter was not at all complimentary about the inns or the horses available to them.'

'I believe the service varies a great deal throughout the land. And how is your sister enjoying London?'

'I have no idea. They have only been there a few days and

Mama's letter was little more than a note to advise me that they had arrived safely. When you go to London,' she added, studying the fingers of her gloves, 'you must be sure to tell Camilla that you travel only with your own horses, she will be most impressed.'

'I have no wish to boast of such things,' he retorted.

'But you wish to gain favour with my sister, do you not?'

The viscount hesitated. He considered the question an impertinence, and a sharp put-down hovered on the edge of his tongue but he held it back. After all, the chit had a point: he very much wanted to see the enchanting Camilla again. He tried for a lighter note.

'What makes you think, that, Miss Symonds?'

'I saw it in your face when you were introduced to her. It is the same with all the gentlemen,' she added kindly. 'You all find my sister irresistible.'

'Squire Woodcote would appear to be the exception,' he retorted, stung by the truth of her observations.

She was not noticeably dashed by his acerbic tone and merely smiled.

'Oh no, but he knows my father would never allow him near Camilla: she is destined to marry an earl at the very least. Or perhaps, if you have great good fortune, she might settle for a viscount.'

Lord Kennington realized with a jolt of surprise that his companion was teasing him. He turned towards her, his eyes narrowed with suspicion, but she returned his look with such an innocent gaze that his anger disappeared. He laughed.

'I do believe, Miss Symonds, that you are roasting me.'

'No, indeed I would not dare,' she said, a laugh quivering in her voice. 'And after your kindness to me, I promise you I shall help you all I can with your suit.'

'Thank you. Perhaps it would be useful to know a little more about your sister, her taste in books, for example, and her favourite flowers. You are frowning, Miss Symonds: surely you can answer these simple questions for me?'

'Yes, of course. Her favourite flowers are bluebells, ever since she was told they matched her eyes, but do not talk to her of books; it is a penance for her to read anything except the society pages of a periodical—' She broke off and fixed her candid brown eyes upon him. 'Do you truly wish to offer for my sister?'

'Well, of course I do!'

'After only a few days' acquaintance?'

'It is nothing of the sort! You know very well we have known each other for years, since we were children.'

'But you did not like her then,' she pointed out to him. 'You thought her silly and teased her because she was frightened of spiders and could not catch a ball.'

'I do not remember that,' he retorted, nettled.

'Well, it was so: in fact, Ned told me you only allowed *me* to play with you when you needed someone to make up the numbers.'

'Yes, well, schoolboys are very thoughtless, you know, and we were very young. Now I can appreciate Miss Camilla for what she is, a most delightful young lady.'

'And very beautiful.'

The viscount smiled.

'Oh yes,' he said softly. 'A veritable diamond.'

By the time they reached Bromsgrove the rain had eased and the cloud had broken up sufficiently to persuade Lord Kennington it would be safe to put down the hood for the last stage of the journey. He slowed as they approached the Swan, a large coaching inn and guided his team through the narrow arch leading to the yard. While Potts directed operations on the curricle, Lord Kennington ushered Lucasta indoors and ordered the landlord to bring them some coffee.

'Will that not delay us?' she asked, as they were escorted to a private parlour.

'A few minutes, perhaps, but we are making good time, and I thought it might refresh you.'

'Thank you, it will.' She took off her hat and cloak. 'Now what is there to laugh at?'

The viscount shook his head, still chuckling.

'Who cut your hair?'

She put her hand up to smooth back the tendrils that had escaped from the velvet ribbon at the nape of her neck.

'I did. I could hardly travel with it hanging down to my waist. Why, is anything wrong?'

'Everything,' he said brutally. 'Make sure you put your hat on and pull your cloak over your hair before we leave here. I would not have anyone look too closely at those rats' tails.'

She pulled the queue over her shoulder, twisting her head to look at it.

'I can see nothing wrong with it.'

'No, which convinces me that you should not be out alone! Let me pour you some coffee.'

She looked at him resentfully, but came forward to take the dish of coffee he was holding out to her. It was hot and strong and she wrapped her hands around the bowl, enjoying the warmth.

'I had not realized how cold I had become,' she said with a little smile.

'The air can be very chill at this time of the year. Will you not sit down?'

'Thank you, sir, but I shall be sitting down in your carriage again very soon.' She wandered over to the window. It overlooked the yard and she could see the viscount's groom standing with a mug of ale in one hand while he directed the stable hands with the other, pointing out various buckles that had not been fastened to his satisfaction. The yard was surprisingly quiet, and she was about to remark upon the lack of custom when another vehicle swept into the yard. It was a curricle, but unlike the viscount's sleek black carriage this one was bright canary yellow. The driver wore a high crowned beaver and a pale surcoat with a froth of capes over his shoulders. Lucasta watched in surprise as he gestured for the stable boys to take his horses. A glance at the little, black-clad figure sitting beside the driver made it clear to her that the gentleman had forsaken his groom for his valet. While the driver made an elaborate show of pulling out his snuff box and helping himself to a couple of pinches, the servant climbed down gingerly from the curricle. He lifted a small leather case from the carriage and began to make his way towards the inn. Amused, Lucasta watched as the man tiptoed across the cobbles, trying to avoid the dirt. He was small and narrow shouldered with a thin, pointed face and shifting, close-set eyes. Little tufts of mousy hair stuck out beneath his hat and, as a tap-boy greeted him and tried to take the leather case, he gathered it to him protectively, his teeth bared in a snarl that made the unfortunate lad step back a pace. His master broke off from barking orders at the stable boys to yell across the yard.

'Damn you, Miesel, get inside and bespeak me some brandy!'

The effect upon the little man was startling: he darted towards the door and Lucasta lost sight of him. She turned from the window with a chuckle.

'Miesel – I think he would be better named weasel! What a funny little man.'

The viscount looked up, one brow raised in enquiry, and she explained. 'A gentleman has arrived with his servant: his valet, rather than his groom. I should think that denotes someone who cares more for his appearance than for his horses.'

He laughed. 'Jacob Potts would agree with you! Come, if you have finished your coffee, we should be on our way. Here.' He walked up to her and pulled her hat more securely onto her head. 'Let me look at you?' His hand beneath her chin forced her to meet his fierce scrutiny and Lucasta found herself growing warm. She was convinced that her cheeks were bright red, but the viscount did not appear to notice. 'Hmm, that will do. Now go out and wait in the curricle while I settle up.'

Pulling her cloak tightly about her, Lucasta hurried out of the room. She was so intent upon keeping her head down that she did not notice the driver of the yellow carriage striding towards the doorway and as she stepped out of the inn she collided heavily with him.

'Damnation, why can't you look where you are going!' A string of coarse oaths followed, drowning Lucasta's apologies. As she tried to step away she found her arm caught in an iron grip. 'Not so fast, you young cub! Do you think you can jostle me and get away with it?'

'Sir, I have said I am sorry—' Lucasta struggled in vain to free herself.

'Well, sorry ain't good enough,' bellowed the man, raising his riding crop. 'What you need is a good whipping!'

'Touch the lad and you will have me to answer to!'

The viscount's voice cut like steel across the yard. Everyone stopped what they were doing and fell silent. Lucasta had braced herself to feel the slash of the whip, but she peeped up now and saw that her assailant was slowly lowering his whip hand and glaring at the viscount with a look of profound dislike upon his heavy features.

'And what has this to do with you, Kennington?'

'The boy is travelling under my protection. If you have a quarrel with him, then you had best take it up with me.'

Lucasta stared at the viscount. She had not realized he could look so menacing. His many-caped driving coat enhanced his already broad shoulders and he filled the wide doorway to the inn. His usually smiling eyes were dark and hard as granite, his mouth a thin line of determination. The grip on her arm slackened and she pulled herself free. Lord Kennington stepped out from the inn doorway and beckoned her to join him. A few strides took her to his side and she felt the immeasurable comfort of his arm placed protectively around her shoulders. 'Well, Bradfield? I heard the boy apologize: will you accept that?'

For a long moment the two men stared at each other, the man called Bradfield glaring angrily, but Lord Kennington's expression had not changed, he still wore that hard, implacable look. She shivered. Eventually Bradfield looked away. He shrugged.

'His apology is accepted, but keep the young cub on a leash, Kennington. If he crosses my path again I'll not be so lenient.'

Obedient to the pressure on her shoulder, Lucasta accompanied Lord Kennington to the curricle where Potts was waiting for them. Silently they climbed up.

'I am sorry,' whispered Lucasta, as the viscount gathered up the reins. 'I did not see him. I did not mean to—'

'I know it.' He laughed as he turned his horses. 'Who would have thought a simple drive to Hansford could be so entertaining!'

Lucasta's anxiety was lessened by his tone, but a glance at

Bradfield's glowering face as they drove out of the yard made her serious again.

'My lord,' she touched his sleeve. 'My lord, he is glaring at you most viciously. I think he would do you harm, if he could.' Her hand was taken in a warm, comforting clasp.

'Think nothing of it, Luke. Sir Talbot Bradfield is a bully and a drunkard. He will not inconvenience you again.'

As they made their way out onto the highway, Lord Kennington asked Lucasta if she objected to riding in the open carriage. She was quick to disclaim, saying cheerfully, 'Oh, I am not cold now. I love to feel the air on my face, and to be able to see so much of the country.'

They drove south from Bromsgrove but soon turned off the main highway onto what was little more than a rutted track, made muddy by the recent rains. It ran through the most empty and wild land Lucasta had yet seen that day: there were no houses in sight, and only the occasional shepherd grazing his flock upon the common. As the afternoon wore on the cloud grew thicker and after a short, golden blaze the sun disappeared for good. Lucasta drew her cloak more tightly about her to keep out the chill wind, and a sudden scrape of metal made her glance back at the groom.

'Just readying the firing piece, miss,' growled Potts, cradling a long-barrelled shotgun in his arms. 'This is a lonely stretch of common.'

'Aye,' agreed the viscount, whipping up his team. 'We are nearing the southern edge now, but we won't tarry here, I think.'

Hardly had the words left his lips than a group of men emerged from the bushes and moved across the road ahead of them. Potts stood up.

'Here we go, my lord. Keep 'em steady.'

'Over their heads, Jacob,' muttered Lord Kennington. 'We only want to scatter them.'

Lucasta watched in horror as one of the figures raised his arm and aimed a pistol at the oncoming carriage, but even as he did so there was a deafening report from the shotgun. The little group ducked and dived to each side of the road as the curricle hurtled towards them.

'That showed 'em,' chuckled Potts as they flew past the men. 'Never knew a footpad to—'

He broke off with a yell and Lucasta swung round to see that one of the men had taken a shot at the curricle as it swept by. Reaching inside her cloak she drew out a pistol, took aim and fired. The viscount swore violently.

'Deuce and the devil! Where did you get that thing?'

'I brought it with me,' said Lucasta, returning the pistol to her pocket. 'Did you think I would set out alone without anything to protect me?'

'And she can use it, too, sir. Fair blew the villain's hat off,' gasped Potts, looking back.

The viscount gave a shout of laughter.

'Miss Symonds, you are a very resourceful young lady.'

'Yes, well, you had best pull up as soon as may be, Adam,' she replied, in a shaking voice. 'Your groom has taken a bullet in his leg.' She took the shotgun from Potts's failing grasp and returned it to its holster, then she snatched off her neck-cloth. 'Here, hold this over the wound: it will help to stem the bleeding until we can bind you up.'

She handed Potts the neck-cloth, trying not to look at the bloody hand that he had clapped over his thigh. The viscount steadied his team and he now risked a glance over his shoulder.

'How badly are you hurt, Jacob? Do you want me to stop or shall I go on to the inn at the edge of the common?'

'Drive on to the Pigeons, my lord,' gasped Potts. 'I can hold on till then. I ain't at death's door yet. And you miss,' he addressed Lucasta, who was still kneeling up on the seat looking back at him. 'You should turn about and sit down properly on that seat. How's his lordship to give his mind to his horses if you are like to fall out o' the carriage at any minute?'

The viscount grinned.

'Definitely *not* at death's door,' he murmured, as Lucasta meekly turned to sit down.

It took them several minutes to reach the Pigeons and Lucasta realized at a glance that this was not one of the usual coaching inns. The yard was surrounded by an assortment of run-down buildings and the lad who came running out of the stable stared in amazement at the magnificent equipage that pulled up before him.

'Quick, boy, take their heads.'

The viscount's order seemed to surprise the boy, who moved uncertainly towards the snorting, head-tossing beasts. At that moment the landlord stepped out of the inn and took in the situation in one glance.

'Look to the horses, Davy, quick now.' He ran forward to help Lord Kennngton lift his groom from the curricle. 'Well now, sir, what's amiss?'

'Footpads on the common,' retorted the viscount. He was supporting the near-unconscious Potts but hesitated and looked back at his team.

Lucasta stepped up.

'You look to your man, my lord. I will see that your horses are stabled properly.' She read the doubt in his eyes and put up her chin, her own eyes glinting. 'I know what to do; you may trust me, sir.'

With a curt nod and a look that told Lucasta he considered he had no choice in the matter, Lord Kennington gave his attention to his injured groom. Orders were barked out, the tap boy was sent running for the surgeon and Potts was carried indoors. Squaring her shoulders, Lucasta turned towards the diminutive stable lad.

'Well, Davy,' she said, in as gruff a voice as she could manage, 'let us take care of his lordship's cattle, shall we?'

CHAPTER SIX

Two hours later Lucasta went in search of the viscount. She was directed to one of the inn's best bedrooms and went in to find Lord Kennington conducting a quiet but earnest discussion with a black-coated man in a grey full-bottomed wig. They were standing to one side of a large bed, where Potts was lying so unnaturally straight and still that for a brief moment Lucasta feared he had not survived.

'He is asleep,' said the viscount, observing her shocked face. 'The landlord has set aside a private parlour for us. Go and wait for me there, Luke, we have almost finished.'

Thus dismissed, Lucasta went off to the little sitting-room hastily vacated by the landlord's family when that shrewd businessman realized that this unexpected guest was prepared to pay handsomely for his comforts. Unable to settle, she whiled away her time ordering supper and stirring the coals until they yielded a cheerful blaze. When Lord Kennington came in some time later she had just finished dragging the little gate-leg table closer to the fire.

'There is such a draught coming from the window I thought we would be more comfortable here,' she explained, pulling a chair up to the table. 'You see our host has already brought us wine, and I have ordered a meal for us. Are you

46

ready to eat now, or do you wish to see the Justice of the Peace first?'

'I am not going to report the attack. I do not wish to draw attention to our situation here.

'Oh.' She digested this. 'Is that because of me?'

'Well, yes, Luke, it is.'

'Oh,' she said again. 'How is Mr Potts?'

'Sleeping now.' The viscount carried a second chair across the room. 'It is only a flesh wound but it is deep, and Jacob has lost a great deal of blood. He is very weak, but the surgeon thinks he will recover well enough if he is allowed to rest for a few days.'

'That is good news.'

The viscount frowned.

'Yes, but it is dashed inconvenient.'

'My lord?'

He gave her an impatient look.

'What am I supposed to do with you?'

'What – what do you mean?'

'It is one thing to take you up and carry you to my godmother's house all in one day, it is quite another for you to spend a night in this inn, alone and unattended.'

She sank down onto the chair she had pulled up to the table.

'I confess I have been so anxious about your groom I had not given a thought to my own situation. But it is not so bad,' she added, trying to smile. 'Everyone here thinks I am a boy and I have told them I am Luke Smith: I thought it best not to use my real name.'

'But if the truth should be discovered we should be in the suds,' he retorted.

'Then we must ensure we are not found out.'

Her reasonable tone was too much for Lord Kennington,

who sat down at the table and dropped his head in his hands.

'What a damnable coil!'

Lucasta regarded him with dismay.

'I am sorry you regard it in that way,' she said stiffly.

He raised his head.

'How else should I regard it? Surely you must see that you cannot stay here with me.'

Lucasta glanced at the clock.

'It is past eight o'clock. Where would you suggest I go?'

With a smothered oath he cast his eyes to the ceiling.

'I wish to heaven I had not taken you up!'

With a sigh he looked across at Lucasta. Her bottom lip began to tremble and she sank her teeth into it, blinking rapidly. It was obvious she was close to tears.

'That is not very gallant of you, my lord,' she said in a small voice. When he did not reply she continued quietly, 'I saw to it that your curricle was cleaned and put in the barn, then I had the bags taken up to the bedroom. And I helped little Davy to rub down the horses and made sure they were bedded down safely for the night.'

'The devil you did! Where did you learn the trade of a stable boy?'

She raised her brows at him and said with a touch of hauteur, 'Ned taught me. He says a good horseman should know how to look after his animals.'

The viscount frowned at her but she did not look away, and there was such a look of determination in her face that his anger evaporated and he gave her a wry smile.

'My apologies, Luke. I am not being very gallant to you, am I?'

'No, sir, but you are anxious, and I know that worry can make any gentleman ill-tempered.'

He chuckled.

'As can hunger. Did you say you have ordered a meal for us? That was well done of you. What do you say to taking a glass of the wine I see over there on the sideboard and we shall leave any decisions on what is to be done until after we have supped?'

Lucasta jumped up immediately and carried the bottle and wine glasses to the table, eager to see harmony restored. The viscount filled two glasses and lifted one in salute.

'So while I have been closeted with Jacob and the surgeon you have seen to my carriage and horses, made this room comfortable and ordered a meal. My compliments Miss – *Master* Smith, you are most resourceful.'

She twinkled at him over the rim of her glass.

'Thank you, my lord.'

A light scratching at the door heralded the entrance of landlady bearing a tray laden with dishes and they watched in silence as she set the meal before them.

'This looks surprisingly good,' remarked the viscount when they were alone again.

'I think our host wishes to impress you. May I help you to a little of the veal pie, Adam, or will you take the spring lamb?'

He smiled inwardly at her use of his name, but he let it go and the meal proceeded pleasantly enough, the only discord coming when the dishes had been cleared and the landlord brought in his finest brandy and two glasses. Lord Kennington immediately ordered small beer to be served to Lucasta.

'But I should like to try a little brandy,' she objected.

He met her challenging look with a bland smile.

'Your father would say you were far too young.'

'Ned was drinking brandy when he was much younger

49

than I,' she hissed as the landlord went away to fetch a jug of beer.

He raised one eyebrow at her.

'And how old are you?' She hesitated, and his lips twitched. 'Well?'

'I am nearly one-and-twenty.'

'Then you are far too young for brandy. Besides, you must keep a clear head if you are to help me decide how we are going to maintain propriety tonight.'

'Yes, I have been thinking about that.' Lucasta rested her elbows on the table and cupped her chin on her hands. 'The landlord told me he has only the two bedrooms, and Potts is in the largest, so I suppose you must share with him.'

'The devil I will!' exclaimed Adam, revolted.

'Well, what do you suggest?'

'I shall sleep in here.'

It was Lucasta's turn to be shocked.

'No! You cannot do that.'

'Why not?'

'Well, there is no bed, for one thing.'

'There is a settle in the corner. That and a few blankets are all I need.'

Lucasta shook her head.

'No,' she said decidedly. 'It would not be right.' Under the viscount's enquiring glance she dropped her eyes and shifted uncomfortably on her chair. 'You – you are a gentleman. You should not be sleeping in here.'

'One night will not kill me.' He broke off as the landlord came back in with large jug and a horn cup which he placed on the table in front of Lucasta. Absently she filled the cup and took a cautious sip.

'There is a truckle bed in the bedchamber,' she murmured, when they were alone again. 'I saw it when I took my bag upstairs – I could sleep in that and you could have the—'

'No!'

His vehemence shocked them both. He reached across the table and caught her hand. 'Luke, I am sorry, I did not mean to sound so out of reason cross with you, but you must see that we are in the devil of a pickle and I would not for the world compromise you further. Tomorrow I shall drive you to my godmother: once you are under her protection you will be safe, but until then we must do what we can to safeguard you. Pray, my dear, help me with this.'

She stared at him across the table, then gave a little smile.

'I am sorry, Adam, I did not mean to be such a trial to you. Tell me what you want me to do.'

He squeezed her hand.

'Good girl. You shall retire soon and be sure to lock your door.'

'And ... you will sleep here?' She looked doubtfully around the little parlour. 'Will that not cause some comment? I believe that in these places it is not unusual for men to share two, three – even four in a bed.'

A smile tugged at the corners of his mouth.

'But we are Quality, Luke,' he said softly, 'and everyone knows that the ways of the Quality are incomprehensible.'

When Lucasta made her way down to the little parlour the next morning she was surprised to find Lord Kennington shaved, dressed and enjoying a hearty breakfast of eggs and ham while the landlord hovered anxiously over him. He welcomed her with a smile, did not rise but waved his fork at her.

'Good morning, Luke. Come and join me, my boy. There is ale here, or our host will find you some coffee, I am sure.'

'Yes, I would like a cup of coffee, if I may,' she murmured, taking her place at the table. When their host had left them alone she added quietly, 'I expected to find you suffering from a lack of sleep.'

'The settle was very hard, I admit, but I have slept in worse places. However, I was not tempted to linger in my makeshift bed and was up betimes to make myself presentable. Unlike you, young man.' He bent a frowning look at Lucasta. 'What is that around your neck?'

She put up her hand to her cravat.

'Is it so very bad? It is a spare neck cloth I packed in my bag. I fear it is a little crumpled, but I did my best.'

'Well, your best falls a long way short of acceptable. Do you not have another?'

'Of course not. I did not expect to need more than one.'

'Good heavens – no self-respecting gentleman would travel without a dozen spare neck-cloths!'

In spite of his harsh words she saw the gleam of mischief in his eyes and her own lips twitched.

'Then I am clearly not a gentleman!'

'If I had not sent all my own baggage on to Coombe Chase I would find you another; as it is, I suggest you wrap your muffler around your neck to cover up that – that sartorial disaster.'

As the landlord came back into the room at that moment she bit back her retort and asked instead after Mr Potts.

'He was awake when I called in upon him this morning and he is anxious to be up and about. The wound looks to be healing well so I plan to take him with us.'

Lucasta looked up, surprised.

'Is that wise, sir? Should he not keep to his bed a little longer?'

The viscount waited until they were alone once more

before replying.

'He should, of course, but I am anxious to be gone. I do not wish to offend our host, but I think Potts will recover more quickly in more – ah – salubrious surroundings. It is not far to Coombe Chase and I hope he will not suffer overmuch on the journey.'

'He must sit beside you in the curricle,' nodded Lucasta. 'And I will occupy the little seat at the back, and handle the yard of tin. I have always wanted to do that!'

Lord Kennington laughed at her.

'What a sad romp you are! Unfortunately, there will be little opportunity for using the horn between here and my godmother's house.'

'But I may sit in the rumble seat?'

'As you wish, although I think Potts may have strong objections!'

Lord Kennington was right, and when the idea was put to Jacob Potts he immediately declared that he was fit as a fiddle.

'Nonsense, man, I would not be moving you at all if there was any help for it, but I have to get Miss Symonds to Coombe Chase and I would rather not leave you behind,' retorted the viscount. 'I did ask the landlord if he had a carriage I could hire, but the only vehicle available is a farm wagon, last used for moving – er – turnips.'

Lucasta, knocking and entering the sickroom in time to hear this, gave a huff of disapproval.

'That would not do at all,' she said. 'You must travel in the curricle, Mr Potts and your injured leg will be supported upon my portmanteau and by pillows that the landlord has been persuaded to sell to his lordship—'

'Oh? And just how much am I paying for these pillows?'

She met his frowning look with a sunny smile.

'Only a few pence, sir. And he assures me they are very *good* pillows, although I would not think they are the quality that you are used to, and I have no doubt we shall throw them away once we are finished with them. . . .'

'Now look, miss, there is no need for all this—'

She put up her hand.

'Not another word, Mr Potts. Lord Kennington is anxious to get you to Coombe Chase so that you can recover properly and to convey you in the curricle is by far the easiest solution for everyone. Now, I have left that little stable boy minding the horses and there is a very chill wind blowing, so I think we should set off as soon as possible. My lord, you will need some help to carry Mr Potts out of the inn: I will ask the tap boy to assist you.' Upon these words she was gone, leaving the groom to stare after her.

The viscount regarded his henchman's scowl and his lips twitched.

'Well, Jacob, do you wish to protest?'

The groom shook his head slowly.

'I'd be as well barking at the moon, m'lord. Who'd've thought that slip of a thing would turn out to be so managing? We've been fair bamboozled, I'm thinking.'

Lord Kennington threw back his head and laughed.

'Aye, Jacob, I think we have.'

CHAPTER SEVEN

Lord Kennington drove his curricle away from the Pigeons some half an hour later, trying to keep a steady pace and avoid any jolting to Potts, who was sitting beside him, his injured leg supported on pillows and wrapped up in a quantity of blankets. For this luxury he had Lucasta to thank, although he looked anything but grateful for the attention he was receiving. The viscount flicked him an amused glance as he pulled out on to the road.

'Cheer up, Jacob, once we get to Coombe Chase I will hand you over to my godmother's people. And we'll get the estate doctor to come and have a look at that wound, too.'

'A jug of home-brewed and a bit o' peace and quiet is all I needs, sir.' He cast a quick look over his shoulder to where Lucasta was sitting in the rumble seat, looking about her with interest. 'Not that I'm complainin'; I know many a master would have gone on and left me to shift for meself.'

'So might I have done if the Pigeons had been a bigger establishment. I fear it is frequented only by the local people who come to the common to graze their animals and gather firewood.'

'And I had no great opinion of the landlady,' put in Lucasta over their shoulders. 'I suspect the sheets were not aired.'

Neither man commented on this dereliction, considering themselves above such womanly concerns and Lucasta, thus chastened, returned her attention to the passing country-side.

It might have been expected that she would be anxious about the forthcoming meeting with the Duchess of Filwood, but concern for Mr Potts's condition was uppermost in her mind and it was not until they had seen the groom carried to a spare bedroom and delivered into the care of the estate doctor that she thought of her own situation. As the viscount led her through the warren of corridors that led from the servants' quarters to the main reception rooms, doubts began to assail her and she wondered aloud if she should perhaps wait in the hall while Lord Kennington apprised his godmother of her presence.

The viscount did not reply, for as they emerged into the great hall the duchess's stately butler came forward to inform them that her grace was awaiting them in the morn-ing-room. The viscount put his arm about Lucasta's drooping shoulders.

'There, you see, Luke, the tale is half-told already. Come along now, it is time to make your bow to my godmama.'

He led the way into the morning-room. Following close behind him, Lucasta peeped past the viscount at the lady waiting to greet them and her spirits sank. The Duchess of Filwood presented a striking figure, dressed in a closed robe of sapphire blue satin embellished at the neck and elbows with a froth of blond lace. Her grey-powdered hair was piled high and topped by a lace cap, adding to her already impos-ing height. However, when Lucasta turned her gaze to the duchess's face she was relieved to see that her blue eyes twinkled with merriment and she was uttering warm words of welcome to the viscount. Lord Kennington took her outstretched hand.

'Your Grace.' He made an elegant bow over her fingers. 'Firstly my apologies for being so late – I had planned to be here yesterday, hard on the heels of my baggage cart.'

The duchess gave a throaty chuckle.

'Punctuality is not something I associate with young gentlemen: I am well aware that there are always temptations on the road, usually a mill or a landlord's daughter! However, this time I understand you were caught up in a true adventure, resulting in your groom taking a bullet in his leg.'

'A flesh wound, ma'am, nothing more. I have left Potts to the tender mercies of your local sawbones, who confirms Potts's own assertion that to restore him to health he requires nothing more than a clean bed and good food. I know he is assured of both under your roof.'

'What was it, footpads?'

'Aye, Your Grace, upon the heath. Potts took a bullet to the thigh but my young friend here gave them their own again, and almost winged one of the villains.' Lord Kennington beckoned to Lucasta. 'Come forward, Luke, and make your bow.'

Nervously Lucasta stepped up, made a flourishing bow and tentatively raised her eyes to her hostess. She suffered something of a shock to find the duchess regarding her with a look of wicked amusement in her eyes.

'Well, Adam, why this masquerade? What mischief are you up to now?'

'You are not deceived, then Godmama.'

'Of course not.'

The viscount laughed.

'You are awake upon every suit, as ever, ma'am.' He drew Lucasta a little closer. 'Your Grace, allow me to present to you Miss Lucasta Symonds.'

'Delighted to meet you, Miss Symonds – no, do not try to curtsey to me in those breeches, child, your bow was elegant enough.' She cast a quick, speculative look towards her godson. 'Is this an elopement?'

'Good God, no!'

Lucasta had been about to disclaim but the viscount's swift utterance made her close her mouth again, a faint blush settling over her cheeks as she listened to his frank explanation of her reasons for running away and how he had come to take her up.

'So you see, Your Grace, it was my intention to bring Miss Symonds to you yesterday. Unfortunately the footpads put paid to my plans. We were obliged to put up at an inn overnight, and now, madam, we are in a devil of a fix, if you will not help us.'

'Then we must see what is to be done. Pray ring the bell, Adam, and we shall take a dish of tea together. I usually rely on Mr Giggs to organize these little luxuries but he is not here.'

'Now you come to mention it, where *is* Giggs?' asked the viscount when he had sent a footman running to the kitchens.

'He is gone to the village to visit the rector. We must be thankful for it: he has a nose for scandal so we must do what we can to keep this from him.' She turned to Lucasta. 'Mr Giggs is a very worthy gentleman sent to live with me by my son, the present duke, who fears that if I am left to my own devices I may get up to mischief and bring his good name into disrepute.' She sighed. 'It is sad to think that my only son has turned out to be such a dull-pickle.'

'Nothing like his parents,' murmured Adam, his smile robbing the words of any offence.

'Nothing at all,' agreed his godmother with feeling. 'His poor father was a sad rake – until he married me, of course. After that he was only a little . . . wild. Perhaps, knowing the world as we did, we were too strict with Charles, but he is sadly lacking in spirit.' She straightened up in her chair. 'But we must not repine, especially when you have brought me such a diversion.'

Lucasta flushed under her smiling look.

'I apologize for the disguise, ma'am, but I thought it would be safer to travel thus.'

'Undoubtedly,' agreed the duchess. 'If one is determined to escape a distasteful marriage one should try to avoid an even more unpleasant fate.' She tapped her fan against her lips, her eyes narrowed in thought. 'Who has seen you in this guise?'

Lucasta swallowed painfully.

'The landlord at the Pigeons, his wife and the stable-boy . . . and your servants, when we brought Mr Potts in.'

'So many? But I have no doubt that they were all taken in by your disguise.'

'*You* were not, ma'am,' ventured Lucasta.

'No, but it was my godson's grinning countenance that put me on my guard.' She took Lucasta's chin between her fingers and turned her face up. 'Hmm, you are a pleasant-enough schoolboy but methinks you would make a much fairer maid.' She looked up at the sound of a scratching on the door. 'Ah, Mr Giggs, you are back at last.'

Lucasta stepped back as a tall, spare gentleman entered the room and made a low bow to the duchess. He was dressed in a plain black coat and breeches and wore a full-bottomed wig of the type worn by doctors and clerics. When he spoke his tone was clipped and precise: Lucasta wondered if he was perhaps a lawyer.

'Your Grace, deepest apologies for my long absence. Mr Williams was indisposed and I was obliged to spend some time comforting his lady.' He drew out a white square of muslin and dabbed at his brow. 'They fear there may be influenza in the village.'

The duchess held up her hand.

'If that is so then come no nearer, Mr Giggs. You will see that my godson and his young friend are come to visit me and I would not have you infect them.'

'I assure Your Grace that I have not—'

'Enough! My dear man I can see already that you are sadly flushed. Tell me that you are not running a temperature.'

'Well, ma'am now you come to mention it I am feeling a little hot. . . .'

'Then get you to your room immediately and send for a hot brick for your feet. Swift action now may well prevent a virulent attack. You shall be attended, sir.'

'Madam, I hardly think—'

'I will not be gainsaid,' her grace interrupted him ruthlessly. 'You must go to bed immediately, Mr Giggs, and stay there until Dr Harbottle gives you leave to get up again.'

'Your ladyship is all goodness, but I cannot neglect my duties so—'

'Nonsense sir, consider it your duty to keep your infection to yourself. Off you go now, man.'

Mr Giggs hesitated a moment more, but the duchess stared at him so fiercely that with a final bow to the company he left the room. She waited until the door was closed again then sank down into her chair and began to fan herself.

'We are safe, I think. He did not look too closely at you, my dear.'

'And will he take to his bed, ma'am?' asked Lucasta, wide-eyed.

'Very likely. The poor man has a morbid fear of illness. It is most useful, when I have had enough of his company, to suggest that he might be ailing. Dr Harbottle will suggest he keeps to his bed for a few days and he will not worry us.'

'He is a tale-bearer,' said Adam scornfully. 'You should turn him off.'

She spread her hands. 'What good would that do? Filwood might foist upon me some poor, impoverished relative and I should be obliged to pity them: at least with Mr Giggs I do not feel in the least sorry for him, and therefore I can laugh at him. But enough of that tiresome man – what are we going to do with *you*, Miss Symonds?'

'We must deliver her to her mama, of course, with all speed,' said the viscount.

'Yes, yes, but the child can go no further today.' She turned to Lucasta. 'Unfortunately, you must keep up this pretence for a while longer: you have been seen by far too many of my staff, and with the exception of Calder, my dresser I would trust none of them with such a secret.'

Lucasta indicated her muddied raiment.

'But, Your Grace, I did not expect to be on the road so long. 'I have no more clothes with me – no boy's clothes, that is.'

'Well, Adam must lend you a clean neck-cloth and as for the rest – we must set it about that in your encounter with the footpads your baggage was lost. I shall put you in the chamber next to my own, and Calder shall see what can be done to clean your clothes tonight.'

The viscount picked up her hand again.

'Your Grace, you never disappoint me.'

She smiled up at him.

'And you, Adam, never fail to entertain!'

*

The duchess ordered an early dinner, saying she would not change her dress, since her young guest was not in a position to do so. Three covers were set at one end of the enormous mahogany dining-table and although Lucasta had been afraid that she would be too nervous to eat, the efforts of her grace's excellent French cook were too tempting to be ignored and with her hostess and the viscount both recommending various dishes to her, she was soon replete.

'You are looking a little tired, young man,' observed the duchess as the final dishes were cleared away. 'Perhaps you would like to retire?' She waited until the last footman had left the room and added quietly, 'It would not be seemly for you to sit over the brandy with Kennington, you know.'

Very much at her ease, Lucasta giggled.

'No indeed, Your Grace. I shall use the excitement of the day as my excuse to leave you.'

'Can you remember your chamber? Do not be afraid to ask for directions: this is a very confusing old house and guests frequently lose their way in the corridors.'

'Thank you ma'am, I believe I shall find it. Goodnight, Your Grace – Lord Kennington.'

The duchess held out her hand, saying languidly, 'You may kiss my fingers . . . there, very elegantly done! Off you go now: I shall have a light supper sent up to you later.' She waited until Lucasta had left the room before requesting the viscount to refill her wineglass.

'What a charming young person! But, Adam, you must tell me the truth now – what do you mean by her, do you have designs upon – er – Luke?'

'Good heavens, no! It was just as I told you, I found her intent upon running away and thought she would be safer with me than wandering alone on the highway.' He grinned suddenly. 'Now if it was her sister. . . .'

'Ah, so your actions are not entirely altruistic. I am relieved,' murmured the duchess, a twinkle in her sharp eyes. 'And is the sister very beautiful?'

He sat back, a little smile playing about his mouth.

'As soft and appealing as a late-summer peach. Her mama has taken her to London for her come-out and I intend to follow her – she is such a beauty that I must act fast before she is snapped up by some other suitor.'

The duchess looked up in some alarm.

'So you are serious this time.'

'Never more so, Godmama. As you remind me often, I am six and twenty: it is high time I found myself a wife. Camilla Symonds is a sweet-natured beauty. Her parentage is good – she comes from one of the oldest families in Shropshire. All in all I think she will do very well for me!'

The duchess raised her glass to him.

'Well then, Adam, I look forward to meeting this paragon!'

CHAPTER EIGHT

In keeping with her charade, Lucasta had been supplied with a nightshirt and a gentleman's dressing gown, both of which were far too big for her and she struggled to move around the elegant guest chamber allotted to her. As promised, a light supper was brought to her room but the servants were under the impression that they were serving a young gentleman and loaded the tray accordingly. Lucasta found no fault with the quantity of cheese and cold meats, but she would have preferred a dish of tea or even a glass of wine to the brandy and ale supplied for her refreshment. However, she did not think it wise to complain and settled down to enjoy her solitary meal. She was curled up in an armchair reading when a narrow door in the panelling opened and the duchess appeared.

'Well now, my dear, do you have everything you need?'

'Y-yes, thank you, Your Grace.' Lucasta struggled out of the chair. 'Calder has taken my coat for brushing and she has promised to have my shirt washed and dry by morning.' She looked down at the silken folds of the dressing gown puddling around her feet. 'I fear I do not match up to Your Grace's usual guests.'

The duchess chuckled.

'You look charming, my dear – except for your hair.'

Lucasta reached up to touch the ragged locks hanging about her shoulders.

'Oh dear, is it so bad? It reached down to my waist, you see, and was far too long for any gentleman so I was obliged to cut it.'

'I quite understand that, however, I think we can improve upon it.' She indicated the door behind her. 'The beauty of this chamber is that it adjoins my own apartments: come through to my dressing-room. I have scissors and a comb there and we shall see what can be done to make you more presentable.'

She led the way through the connecting doors into a high-ceilinged room decorated in shades of cream and pink, illuminated by numerous candles.

'Do you like it? I had it decorated to my own taste when I first moved here. I was newly widowed, you see but I have never liked sombre colours.' She gently pushed Lucasta down on to the stool near the dressing-table and lifted her hair in one hand. 'Dear me,' she said, a slight tremor in her voice, 'did you cut this in the dark?'

'Well, I could not quite reach,' admitted Lucasta. 'I was obliged to pull it over my shoulder and I think perhaps I was a little careless.'

'Yes, I can quite see that. Well, let me see what I can do.'

When Miss Symonds went downstairs the following morning she entered the breakfast-room with something very like a swagger. A quick glance around assured her that only Lord Kennington was present and she said, dimpling, 'Well, my lord, what do you think?'

The viscount had risen upon her entrance and he regarded her now with a decided twinkle in his grey eyes.

'You look very smart, Master Luke.'

'Thank you, my lord. My coat has been brushed and pressed, my shirt washed and my hair cut to a neatness. I am very respectable now, am I not?'

Adam watched her preening herself before the mirror. There was a definite charm about her in her old-fashioned frock-coat. Her hair, freshly cut and scooped back into a queue, was the colour of liquid honey in the morning light. His lips twitched.

'You are a veritable coxcomb. Sit down and break your fast before you wear out the mirror.'

She came to the table, a faint flush suffusing her cheeks. He laughed.

'No, no, I am merely teasing you, Luke. You look very well, I promise you. Would you like me to order you some coffee?'

'Yes, thank you.' She took a seat opposite the viscount and helped herself to a slice of bread and butter. 'Shall we go on to London today, sir?'

'No, it is Sunday: I never travel on a Sunday. Besides I fear one of my bays is a little lame, and without Potts to look at her I think I shall let her rest another day.'

'Oh dear. And if she should indeed prove to be lame?'

'I have no doubt the duchess will allow me to use one of her teams. Do not look so worried, Luke, I shall get you to London in a day or so, never fear.'

'Thank you, my lord.'

He looked up.

'My lord? Why so formal? I have grown used to you calling me Adam.'

She blushed but did not reply for at that moment the footman opened the door for the duchess to enter, followed by a servant bearing a fresh pot of coffee. Morning greetings were exchanged and the duchess took her seat.

'Poor Mr Giggs is no better today,' she informed them solemnly. 'I am afraid we must amuse ourselves.'

'I must go to the stables to check on my horses,' said Adam. 'And I want to see how Potts goes on. After that I am at your disposal for the rest of the day. What would you like to do, Luke? A little shooting, perhaps, or we could play billiards. . . .'

The duchess dismissed her servants with a word.

'I think not,' she continued quietly. 'Luke's disguise makes her no less a lady, Adam, and as such I must not allow her to be alone with you. Pray do not argue, sir: believe me, I would not have either of you compromised. I think it would be best if Luke spent the day in my company. You, Adam, may amuse yourself as best you may.'

Lucasta did not dare to argue with her hostess, but the look she cast Lord Kenington was eloquent enough to make him laugh out loud.

'Poor Luke, there is no need to be so dismayed. You need not think the duchess will keep you yawning over your needlework all day. If I know my godmother she will have much more interesting ways to entertain you!'

She did not look convinced, but when they all met up again shortly before the dinner hour it was clear that Lucasta and the duchess were already firm friends. They were seated together before the fire and as Lord Kennington entered the room Lucasta turned an animated countenance towards him.

'Oh, Adam, we have had such fun today! Madam Duchess drove me to church in her phaeton. It is so high I could see over all the hedges and walls! Then we went to visit Her Grace's gamekeeper – one of his spaniels has whelped and we were allowed to see the litter. There was the most adorable little bitch with one white ear, smaller than all the others and not at all so forward. Madam Duchess says they will all need homes, but if I am going to London it would not be quite fair to take a pup with me, would it?'

'No indeed,' he replied. 'Nor would it be fair to take such a young creature away from its mother.'

She gave a sigh.

'No, I quite see that, so I have quite given up the idea of taking her with me, but Madam Duchess says that if she is not homed by the end of the season I make take her back to Shropshire with me.'

'Not in my carriage!'

She laughed at him.

'No, of course not. I shall be travelling with Mama and Camilla. Madam Duchess says we may call in on our way to see if the puppy is unclaimed. And it is very likely that she will still be here, because she is so much smaller than the others and not half so pretty, is she, Madam Duchess?'

The duchess smiled and threw a swift, mischievous look at her godson.

'I fear she is overshadowed by her siblings.'

'And what of your day, sir?' said Lucasta as the viscount took a seat beside her. 'Did you see Jacob, will he be well enough to travel tomorrow?'

'I am afraid not. The wound is healing well but it will be better if he rests the leg for a few more days yet. We shall have to go on without him.' He lowered his voice a little. 'I have set it about that I am taking Luke to Droitwich where he can pick up a coach.'

'Excellent.' The duchess nodded approvingly. 'Thus Master Smith can disappear into the north country. I shall dispatch Calder shortly before you set off so that you can take her up on the road – she will then act as chaperon until you reach London. Once Luke is safely restored to her mama, Calder shall purchase her ticket on the mail coach to return here.'

Lucasta looked from the duchess to Lord Kennington, her eyes bright with unshed tears.

'I really do not know how to thank you both. You have been so kind to me.'

The duchess waved aside her thanks.

'Nonsense child, I have enjoyed having you to stay and I hope we shall have the pleasure of entertaining Miss Lucasta Symonds here at some future date.'

A quiet dinner was followed by an early night and the duchess was present to say goodbye the next morning. The viscount refused to allow his godmother to venture out of doors because of the chill wind and they took their leave in the echoing marble hall. Impulsively, Lucasta stepped forward to kiss the duchess's scented cheek.

'I shall not forget your kindness, Madam Duchess,' she whispered, her voice breaking.

The duchess pulled her closer, and Lucasta found herself enveloped in a warm embrace.

'Dear child, I have grown very fond of you, even in this short time. There, there, go along with you.' The duchess patted her shoulder. 'We shall meet again, I am sure. Off you go now. God speed, Adam, and take care of Master Smith!'

'You may be sure I will, Your Grace. Tell Potts to join me in London as soon as he is able.'

They climbed into the curricle, the stable lad holding the horses jumped aside and they set off down the drive at a cracking pace. Lucasta leaned over the back of the seat to take a last look at Coombe Chase.

'I do like your godmama, Adam.' She turned and sank back onto her seat with a sigh. 'Do you think she will let me visit her again one day?'

'Very likely. When she likes someone she will go to any lengths for them and she was very taken with you. Now,' he said, whipping up his team, 'we must find the estimable Calder, who should be waiting for us somewhere on this road, then we can set about losing young Master Smith.'

CHAPTER NINE

Two days later a tired and bone-weary Lucasta arrived in London. She had found the journey from Coombe Chase far less enjoyable and put this down to the presence of the duchess's formidable dresser. Calder took her duties as chaperon very seriously, sitting silently between her charge and the viscount and making all but the most necessary conversation impossible. At the inn where they were obliged to put up for the night she instructed Lucasta to wrap herself up in her cloak and she bundled her into her room with instructions for supper and breakfast to be sent up, and when Lucasta was escorted back to her seat in the curricle the following morning the viscount observed drily that a chance observer was more likely to suspect a kidnap than an elopement.

When they arrived in Sophia Street, Lucasta realized belatedly that she had no idea which of the houses had been hired by her mama, but here the duchess's redoubtable dresser proved her worth: a few knocks, a few discreet enquiries and Mrs Symonds's direction was discovered.

'Would you like me to come in with you?' asked the viscount, as Lucasta climbed down from the curricle.

'Thank you, my lord, but that will not be necessary,' put in Calder briskly. 'Miss Symonds is safe enough in my care. Besides there's no one to look after your horses.'

She stepped up to the door and banged the knocker loudly. Lucasta looked back at the viscount.

'I really am very grateful to you, my lord.'

'Think no more of it. I shall call upon you in a few days to see how you go on.' He touched his hat. 'Good day to you, Miss Symonds.'

With a flourish of his whip he set off along the street. Lucasta watched him drive away and pulled her cloak more firmly around her, feeling suddenly bereft.

Moments later she was standing in an elegant morning-room while a lofty butler sent a note to Lady Symonds. She looked across at Calder, standing impassively in one corner, and gave her a nervous smile.

'I am sure we will be able to find you a room for the night – it is too late now for you to set off for Coombe Chase.'

'Thank you miss,' came the civil reply. 'I believe the mail coach leaves early each morning so a little supper and a comfortable bed would be most welcome. Also, I should like to know that you are settled before I take my leave of you. So that I may report back to my mistress,' she added quickly, lest Lucasta should think her capable of any sort of kindness.

'Lucasta – it *is* you! When I was told you had arrived I thought there must be some mistake!' Lady Symonds hurried into the room, Camilla close behind her. 'Has there been some sort of accident? Is it Papa?'

'Papa was quite well when last I saw him,' replied Lucasta. 'It is quite complicated, however. Before I explain, will you give orders for rooms to be prepared? This is Calder, by the way, the Duchess of Filwood's personal maid. She will only be staying for one night, but I shall require a room for a much longer stay, if you will permit me.'

'Yes, yes, of course,' Lady Symonds nodded, looking very bewildered and Lucasta took it upon herself to instruct the butler, who was standing at the door with a look of the liveliest curiosity on his face. Once he and Calder had withdrawn, Lucasta tutted. 'Oh dear – should I have told him to set another place for dinner? But he will know to do that, surely?' She turned towards her mother and sister, who were still standing in the middle of the floor, staring at her. She quelled a sudden desire to laugh and said instead, 'Shall we all sit down?'

As she sank into a chair her cloak fell open to display her raiment.

'Lucasta,' said her mother in a voice of precarious calm, 'What are you doing in Town, dressed as a boy and, and accompanied by a – a duchess's personal maid?'

'Have you received no word from Papa? No? Well, that is very odd, for I left him a note explaining what I was going to do, but perhaps he did not think he could explain himself properly in a letter.'

'Lucasta,' burst in Camilla, 'if you do not tell us exactly what is happening I shall fall into hysterics!'

'I have run away,' she said simply.

'Oh good heavens!' Lady Symonds sank back into her chair and began to ply her fan vigorously.

'I mean,' continued Lucasta, considering her words, 'I have run away from Papa, who was going to force me to marry Squire Woodcote.'

'What?' Lady Symonds dropped her fan and sat bolt upright, her colour fluctuating alarmingly.

Lucasta nodded.

'Squire Woodcote came to dinner and I overheard them

talking: the squire had procured a special licence and Papa planned to call in the parson the very next day to carry out the ceremony.'

She paused. So much had happened that the repugnance she had felt upon discovering her father's plans had faded and she could discuss the matter quite calmly. Camilla, however, was regarding her in horror.

'But Squire Woodcote is so *old.*'

'That does not prevent him wanting a young bride,' retorted Lucasta.

Camilla shuddered.

'What a disgusting idea. Why, the last time he came to call he sat next to me on the sofa and tried to paw me. It was horrible and Mama told Papa he must either forbid him the house altogether, or insist that he leave me alone.'

'Well I wish you had told him to leave *me* alone, too, Mama,' retorted Lucasta.

'But I did not know – that is, I did not think he had any interest in you,' cried her mother.

'I would not be surprised to learn that Papa had put the idea in his head.'

'Lucasta!' gasped Camilla. 'You cannot say such things about Papa.'

'And why not? We all know that Papa sees us only as chattels, goods to be turned into profit.'

'It is true that we want you both to marry well,' put in Lady Symonds, her cheeks very red, 'but I never wanted you to be unhappy. Oh drat the man, how dare he do this? He deliberately waited until I was out of the way. No wonder he has not written to tell me what has occurred; he would not dare! Only wait until I write to him, I shall give him a piece of my mind—'

'Yes, yes, Mama, that is all very well, but we have not yet

heard how Lucasta comes to be here, and accompanied by a lady's maid.'

'Calder is personal dresser to the Duchess of Filwood,' said Lucasta. 'I was a guest of the duchess for a few days, after I had shot a footpad and—' She broke off, biting her lip at her audience's astonished looks. 'I think I had best tell you the whole.'

'. . . so here I am,' said Lucasta when she had finished her story. 'I must throw myself upon your mercy, Mama, although I think it only fair to tell you that if you insist I go back to Shropshire I shall run away again, to Kent this time, and live with Ned.'

No one attended to her. Camilla said wonderingly, 'Lord Kennington brought her here, Mama. Do you think he did it for my sake?'

'Oh, undoubtedly,' replied Lady Symonds. 'Lucasta says he has promised to call: when he does we must be ready, my love, and you must be suitably grateful for his rescuing your sister.'

'Since I was the one who shot at the footpad you could say that *I* rescued *him*,' argued Lucasta.

She was ignored. Her mother paced up and down the room, tapping her fan against her hand.

'Well, now you are here, Lucasta, we must clothe you.'

'I do have one gown in my portmanteau, Mama. I would have worn it, but Calder thought it safer for me to travel as a boy than to risk comment. . . .'

'Then that must suffice for tonight but tomorrow we shall take you shopping: it must be early, in case Lord Kennington should call. Of course, until you are fit to be seen you must keep to your room except for meals – and we must find you a maid. Anne is far too busy looking after

Camilla to bother with you.'

Lucasta let her run on, thankful that she was not to be turned out of the house. She went to her bed that night tired but happy, her only worry being that if the viscount called the next day, she might not be allowed to see him.

After driving away from Sophia Street, Lord Kennington made his way to the stables that enjoyed his patronage while he was in Town. Without Potts, he was obliged to give his own instructions to the stable lads and it took him some time to arrange for the housing of his curricle. The hour was therefore advanced by the time he reached his rooms in Wardour Street and he grinned at the look of shock upon his valet's face as he ran up the stairs.

'Well, Gretton, had you given me up for another day?'

'No, my lord, that is—'

'Do not stand there gawping at me, man. Go and lay out my black coat; I must change before I can go to my club to dine.' He broke off when realized his valet was not alone on the landing. A tall gentleman in a dark coat and bagwig stood behind him and the viscount could see two more figures standing in the shadows.

'Do we have visitors, Gretton?'

'Not *visitors*, as such, sir . . .' the valet tailed off unhappily, and the gentleman in the bagwig stepped forward.

'Am I to understand that you are Lord Kennington, sir?'

'I think you may understand that,' replied the viscount. He had reached the landing by now and paused to strip off his gloves, a faint, questioning lift to his brows.

'I also understand that you have returned from Shropshire, my lord, by way of Bromsgrove and Hansford. That was on Friday, was it not, my lord?'

'Aye, that is so. May I ask where this is leading?'

'Aye, sir. On Friday last, Sir Talbot Bradfield was shot on Hansford Common. We have a witness who says you murdered him.'

CHAPTER TEN

When Lord Kennington did not call in Sophia Street the following day Lady Symonds was disappointed but not surprised.

'Depend upon it, my loves,' she said to her daughters, 'he will not want to seem too eager in his suit.'

However, when another morning passed without a visit she was less sanguine and even inclined to be indignant.

'We have stayed indoors particularly that we might not miss him,' she grumbled, 'and this is how he repays us.'

'I thought we stayed in because I had nothing decent to wear,' put in Lucasta.

'That may have been another reason, but you know we decided my tawny silk would do very nicely for you now we have let down the hem. You shall wear it to Lady Redwater's rout tonight. We have waited long enough for Lord Kennington, he must now take pot luck upon finding us at home, for we really have no interest in him.'

'And as you said, Mama, we might hear news of him at Lady Redwater's,' said Camilla, ruining the effect of her mother's studied indifference.

*

Lucasta was as eager as her mother to go out: she, too, had been expecting the viscount to call and was surprised at the depth of her disappointment. It was therefore with a feeling of pleasurable anticipation rather than her usual trepidation that she made her preparations and allowed her mother's coiffeuse to arrange her hair, concealing its shorter length with artful curls. They arrived at Lady Redwater's fine town house in good time and Lady Symonds introduced her eldest daughter with a smooth explanation of her sudden appearance in Town. Then, flanked by Camilla and Lucasta, she launched herself into the company, alert for news of the viscount.

They had not been in the room five minutes before they heard his name. Lady Symonds immediately turned to the speaker.

'You were talking of Lord Kennington, I believe, sir: is he not here tonight? I made sure to see him. . . .'

The gentleman looked at her in surprise.

'My dear ma'am, you will look for him in vain, I fear.'

'It is best is you do not look for him at all,' tittered the lady on his arm. Observing Lucasta's puzzled look she leaned closer and whispered, 'He has been clapped up.'

'Never was I so taken in,' the gentleman shook his head. 'Why, I was going to offer him my black mare, but not now, not now!'

'Why, what has he done?' asked Lady Symonds, looking around in astonishment.

'Why the fellow's a murderer!'

'No!'

The gentleman turned to Lucasta, shaking his head at her.

'I know, Miss Symonds, it was a shock to us all, but it is beyond doubt. There are witnesses.'

Her mouth felt dry. She forced herself to speak calmly.

'Does anyone know the detail?'

'Aye, 'tis all over Town. He waylaid Sir Talbot Bradfield and shot him dead.'

Camilla gave a small shriek. Lucasta grew cold. She remembered the driver of the yellow curricle, recalled his loud bullying voice and the malevolent glare he had given Adam as they drove away from the inn at Bromsgrove. Surely Adam had not – she could not contemplate such a thing. Clutching her fan tightly to disguise her shaking fingers, she said in a whisper, 'When – when was this?'

'Friday last, in broad daylight as I understand it. Of course, they have him safe in Newgate now.'

'Last Friday, then it cannot be. I—'

'My dear, there is a tear in your gown. Come now: we must see to it before it becomes too noticeable.' Lady Symonds caught Lucasta's arm and bore her away, Camilla hurrying along behind her.

'We must go to the magistrates,' hissed Lucasta. 'I must tell them I was with Lord Kennington last Friday. I can vouch for him.'

'You will do no such thing,' muttered her mother, drawing her rapidly through the crowded room.

'But Mama!'

'Hush, now, until we are alone.' Lady Symonds drew her daughters towards an empty sofa. 'Let us sit for a moment and consider.'

'There is nothing to consider,' whispered Lucasta. 'We must go, immediately.'

'There is *everything* to consider!' her mother contradicted her. 'How would it look if we rushed away this very minute? No, Lucasta, we must stay and learn what more we can about this dreadful affair.'

Lucasta realized that a crowded assembly was not the best place to argue with her mother and held her peace, but the next few hours were unbearably difficult. Everyone was talking of Lord Kennington's arrest and conjecture was rife about the reasons for the crime, from gambling debts to amorous intrigues. As the evening wore on Lucasta's spirits sank even lower, for everyone seemed ready to believe the viscount was guilty, and when she tentatively suggested there could be some mistake heads were shaken, and the word 'witnesses' was thrown at her until she was ready to scream. By the time the carriage was ordered for their journey back to Sophia Street she had developed a sick headache, and sank back into her seat in the darkened carriage with a sigh of relief.

'What a dreadful evening,' exclaimed Camilla, squeezing in beside her. 'So dull – all anyone wanted to talk of was the murder.'

'But no one seems to know very much about it,' sighed Lucasta. 'There is a great deal of gossip and speculation, but very little real information. You must let me speak to the magistrate, Mama.'

'That is out of the question.'

Lucasta peered through the darkness, trying to make out her mother's face.

'But I was with Lord Kennington on Friday, I can prove that he is innocent!'

'Can you? Do you think the revelation that you were traipsing around the country with the viscount, unchaperoned, would do anything to help his case? Everyone would conclude that you were his mistress. Your reputation would be ruined and nothing you said in Lord Kennington's defence would be believed – more likely you would be clapped in Newgate with him!'

The truth of her mother's words dowsed Lucasta like cold water. Hot tears pricked her eyes.

'But I must try,' she whispered. 'I must do *something*.'

'You must do nothing,' insisted Lady Symonds. 'If Lord Kennington thought your evidence could help him I have no doubt the magistrate would have sought you out by now. Be thankful the viscount is too much of a gentleman to drag your name into this matter.'

'But he is innocent, and I know it, so—'

'Lucasta, if your father was an earl then we might be able to carry off such a scandal, but you *cannot* admit that you were with Lord Kennington without bringing the whole family into disrepute. You saw for yourself tonight how everyone has turned against him already: would you range yourself on his side?'

'Yes I would, because he is not a murderer!'

'If that is the case then justice will be done and he will be acquitted.'

'But Mama—'

'Enough!' Lady Symonds shrieked and put her hands up to cover her ears. 'Lucasta, would you ruin Camilla's chances of a good marriage as well as your own? There is nothing useful you can do in this, and I will *not* allow you to jeopardize Camilla's season.'

'No, I think you are being very selfish, Lucasta.' Camilla added her voice to the argument. 'If you admit the truth you will make our family a laughing stock.'

The carriage came to a halt outside their house and in the dim flare of the torches Lucasta could see the closed look on her mother's face.

'Camilla is right,' said Lady Symonds. 'You would ruin us all to no purpose, and then I doubt even Squire Woodcote would marry you!'

CHAPTER ELEVEN

Viscount Kennington had heard much of Newgate but he had never expected to experience it for himself. Looking round his cell, he reflected ruefully that he had lived in worse lodgings. A deep purse ensured that he had a room to himself with modest comforts, although the smell of dirt and decay that permeated the building reminded him constantly of his surroundings. He had refused Gretton's pleas to be allowed to accompany him, saying he could be of more use outside the walls than within, but as he prepared to face his second day in prison the idea of a prolonged incarceration was very daunting. He lay on the hard bed with his hands linked behind his head and watched the first grey fingers of dawn light creep into the room. It was too soon to despair: once the city was awake his lawyer would be at work again on his behalf, and Gretton would be returning shortly with a fresh change of clothes for him. He heard the faint tap, tap of footsteps in the stone corridor. Heeled shoes – a female. His mouth twisted. At this hour of the morning she would be leaving some prisoner's cell and most likely a couple of guineas richer for her trouble. He was surprised therefore when the footsteps stopped outside his door. He sat up, frowning, as the keys rattled in the lock. The gaoler coughed and spat before announcing, 'Visitor for 'ee.'

The door opened and a figure totally enveloped in a black cloak glided into the room. The viscount got to his feet, staring, but the figure did not move until the gaoler had retreated once more, then two small, gloved hands reached up and pushed back the hood of the cloak.

'Lucasta!' Lord Kennington stared at her. 'What the devil are you doing here?'

She gave him a wobbly smile.

'That is a very poor greeting, my lord.'

'You should not be here.'

'I had to come, as soon as I learned what had happened to you.' She put out her hands to him. 'Oh Adam, what is being done to help you?'

He took her hands and guided her to a chair – the only chair in the room – masking his own concerns in his efforts to reassure her.

'Everything possible. You know I am not guilty, it is merely a matter of proving it.' He spoke lightly, squeezing her fingers and releasing them as he resumed his seat on the edge of the bed. Her expression did not alter; her brown eyes were fixed upon him with a painful intensity.

'The man who . . . died,' she said slowly. 'He was the one you quarrelled with at Bromsgrove?'

'Yes.'

'Will you tell me what you know? I have heard nothing but rumours.'

'Word did not take long to spread, then.'

She coloured slightly.

'Yes. I am sorry.'

'Nay, why should you be sorry? And is everyone ready to hang me?' He gave a savage laugh. 'But of course they are. They will all be willing to think the worst of me!'

'Not everyone, Adam!'

'No? Then tell me, does your family know you are here? No, I thought as much. And would they approve? Your face gives me my answer. I cannot blame them for that. It is folly for you to be here, Lucasta.'

Two spots of angry colour flamed on her cheeks.

'It is not! I am as much involved in this as you, so I would very much appreciate you telling me what you are supposed to have done!' She glared at him, such determination in her face that at last he uttered a soft laugh and nodded.

'Very well, I will tell you what I know. When we left Bradfield at the Swan it would appear he continued to rail against me, and the landlord heard him say that he knew my direction and would come after me. He set off about an hour afterwards, with his valet beside him. Some time after this the valet was beating down the door of one of the farms that adjoins the northern edge of the common, saying they had been attacked by footpads.'

'The same ones that attacked us!'

'Possibly. Let me finish. The farmer and two of his farmhands accompanied the valet back to the carriage. Bradfield was lying on the ground beside it. He was dead. His dressing case had been forced open: the valet said that Bradfield had been carrying a valuable emerald necklace to Town. It would appear to have been stolen.'

'A necklace! But—'

The viscount held up his hand. 'Let me finish the whole, Lucasta. The magistrate was summoned and it seems he put some effort into his investigations. His enquiries eventually led him to the Pigeons. You will imagine how our presence there would look – Jacob injured and the description of a young man named Smith who has since vanished – at any rate the magistrate thought it far too suspicious and came to London in search of me.'

'But surely you explained to him that we had been set upon by footpads!'

'Of course, but you will recall that at the time I declined to report the matter. Bradfield was found with a pistol in his hand: it had been fired, and the magistrate is convinced that it was this weapon that wounded Jacob.' He shrugged. 'It is assumed that following my quarrel with Bradfield, we waylaid him on the common, killed him and robbed him to make it appear the work of common thieves.'

'Perhaps it was,' said Lucasta. 'Mayhap it was the same footpads that tried to rob us. If we could find them—'

'And how do you propose to do that, will you go back to Hansford and ask everyone you meet if they are in the habit of robbing travellers?'

'No, of course not, but there must be ways.' She frowned. The viscount was silent, watching her. It was no small comfort to know that her concern was all for him. At last she spoke again.

'The other point that does not make sense is the necklace. It was in a dressing case, you say? I remember the valet carrying just such a case into the Swan. I thought at the time it must be very important for him to bestow so much attention on it. It was not a large item, so why would anyone break it open; why not take the whole case?'

'That thought had occurred to me.'

Her brown eyes widened. 'Unless the thief knew it was there! Adam – what if Bradfield was killed for the necklace?'

'It is possible. I will put that to my lawyer when he comes in later today. He is trying to persuade them to grant me bail, then I shall be able to pursue my own enquiries.'

Lucasta twisted her hands together.

86

'Adam, would it help if you told them that – that I was the young man?'

'Not at all,' he retorted. 'In fact, it would complicate matters exceedingly.'

'That is what Mama said when I suggested it.' She sighed. 'But I feel so *helpless*, knowing you are innocent and not being able to do anything about it.'

'Knowing you can vouch for me is help enough for the present,' he said, smiling at her. 'At least your sister and mother need not doubt my innocence. Poor Camilla, how distraught she must be. Pray tell her – ah, but no one knows of your visit,' He smothered a sigh and after a moment shook himself free of his depressing thoughts. 'And no one must discover that you have been here, Luke.' He rose and reached out to draw Lucasta to her feet. 'Now, it is time you were gone: you are too careless of your reputation, Lucasta. But I *am* grateful for your coming here, never doubt that .' He kissed her cheek before pulling her hood over her head. 'Make sure you are not recognized leaving this place.'

He banged on the door, and a shuffling step was heard. He took a last look at the shrouded figure in front of him and was aware of a feeling of desolation. He put out his hand, as if to hold her, then let it fall again. With a slight inclination of the head, the hooded figure turned and left the room without another word.

CHAPTER TWELVE

The breath-catching nervousness did not leave Lucasta until she was safely in her room again. It was still early and she passed only an incurious lackey on her way through the house. She felt very tired, and slightly depressed; after all, what had she achieved? Adam had said there was little she could do to help him and her slender purse was empty: she had bribed her maid not to tell anyone of her absence, then there had been a similar inducement to the footman who accompanied her. An extra charge had to be agreed before the hackney carriage would wait for her outside the gaol and as for the rest, it had disappeared into the clutching fist of the turnkey: he had demanded payment for every door unlocked on the way to Adam's cell. She glanced at the little bracket clock on the mantel, it was not yet nine: her mama and Camilla rarely left their rooms until ten so she had plenty of time to change into a morning gown and while she did so her thoughts drifted back over her visit to Newgate. Adam was convinced that she should not admit her involvement in the whole affair, but knowing he was innocent was not enough, she wanted to prove it. Remembering what he had told her, it seemed to Lucasta that the valet held the key to the matter. He must have seen the attackers and would be able to explain to the magistrates that it could not have been Lord Kennington After all, there could be no disguising the viscount's tall figure in its drab driving coat and fashionable beaver hat: no footpad would appear thus.

Another problem presented itself: how was she to contact the man? She could not approach him and there was no one in her mother's household whom she would trust with the task. The problem occupied her thoughts for the rest of the day, causing Camilla to complain that her sister was no company at all.

'You are very stupid and dull today, Lucasta,' she cried petulantly. 'I vow I am out of all patience with you: you will be a poor companion at the tea gardens today.'

'Then perhaps it would be best if I did not come with you!' retorted Lucasta, her frayed nerves giving way.

However, Lady Symonds would not hear of her remaining behind and Lucasta was obliged to put on a smile with her new gown and to take her place in the party of pleasure.

With Sir Oswald remaining at Oaklands, Lady Symonds was obliged to rely upon her friends whenever a male escort was required, but there was never any shortage of gentlemen willing to accompany the beautiful Camilla and on their visit to the tea gardens in Chelsea they were accompanied by two respectable young gentlemen whom Lady Symonds relied upon to maintain propriety. Lucasta was relieved to find that she was not expected to contribute much to the conversation since both the gentlemen were besotted with Camilla and she was able to lose herself in her own thoughts as they all strolled through the gardens. It was very early in the season but an exceptionally mild March day had brought out the crowds. At one particularly busy intersection of paths they found themselves jostled on all sides and Lucasta jumped when someone close behind whispered her name.

'A note for you.'

A callused hand was holding out a screw of paper. She took it, glancing up at the figure as she did so, but the man was huddled inside a worn surcoat with muffler wound around his chin and his hat pulled low over his eyes, effectively disguising him.

All Lucasta's conjecture and curiosity had to be contained until she could drop behind her party. Then, while Lady Symonds and Camilla laughed and joked with their escorts, she unfolded the paper. It contained a short message, written in an untidy, ill-formed hand. Lucasta read it and stopped in surprise. Crumpling the paper in her hand she looked around quickly, fearful that she was being observed, but nothing had changed, the two gentlemen were gallantly vying for Camilla's attention while her mother looked on fondly. Lucasta put a hand on her mother's shoulder and murmured her excuse.

'No, do not come with me, Mama,' she added. 'I shall not go far, and it is more important that you prevent Camilla's swains from behaving far too free.'

She could not have chosen a better reason for Lady Symonds to remain with the main party: Camilla might laugh and flirt with her escorts but her mama must make sure there was no hint of impropriety. Smiling to herself, Lucasta slipped away. Within moments of taking a quieter path she heard a voice close behind her.

'There's an empty arbour to your right, miss.'

She turned without hesitation and stepped into the leafy shelter. The figure huddled in the surcoat followed her. Lucasta stared at him, her head on one side and a questioning look in her eyes until the figure lifted his chin free of the muffler. She nodded.

'As I thought. Jacob Potts.'

The groom grinned.

'I didn't think there'd be any fooling you, miss.'

'If nothing else your limp would give you away,' she replied. 'How is your leg now, Jacob?'

'Improving, miss, but it gets a bit painful if I walks too much. I might have stayed with her grace if the law hadn't been on my tail.'

'Oh heavens!' Lucasta sank down onto the bench and put one nervous hand to her throat. Jacob gave a grim little smile.

'Aye, came to arrest me, they did. The magistrate turned up, snoopin' around, but her grace gave 'im short shrift, soon sent 'em all packing. But I didn't want her grace to get into trouble so I ups and comes to London.'

'But surely it is even more dangerous for you to be here.'

'Oh, I haven't been to Wardour Street, nor to the stables neither, knowing that they was waiting to clap me up. But I remembered your direction, miss, and I have been outside since dawn, waitin' for a chance to talk with you.'

'But you could not have followed me here on foot.'

'No, miss, I had to take a hackney carriage.'

She reached for her reticule.

'Then you must let me reimburse you. . . .'

He quickly put out his hand, saying in a shocked voice, 'It ain't come to that yet, miss, that I can't pay me own way.'

He sounded so fierce that she immediately closed her reticule. Remembering the state of her own finances, she could not help feeling slightly relieved. He continued slowly, 'I was thinking, miss, that since my lord was so wondrous great with Miss Camilla, he might have sent a message to her, saying how he goes on?'

'No. At least, if he has done so I have not heard of it.' She paused. 'However, I – um – I saw Lord Kennington this morning.'

'You never did! But he's in Newgate!'

She coloured.

'Yes. I bribed the gaoler to let me in. I cannot tell you very much, only that Lord Kennington seemed well and was expecting his lawyer to arrange bail for him very soon.'

'Well, he hasn't managed it yet,' growled Potts. He tapped his nose. 'Just cos I haven't visited Wardour Street doesn't mean I ain't in touch with Gretton, and the word from him late this morning was that me lord is still clapped up and like to remain so.'

Lucasta sighed.

'Oh Jacob, we must do something!'

'Aye, but what?'

For a while they were silent, watching the crowds strolling past in the warm spring sunshine. At last Lucasta nodded.

'I think it is the valet who holds the key to this.' She sat up, suddenly resolute. 'We must find him and talk to him; make him see that somehow the magistrate has been misled into thinking the viscount is guilty. If he would but talk to the authorities again then all would be well.'

'Then I'll find him. miss. Do you happen to know his name?'

She frowned.

'I know I heard it . . . it was very like weasel – Miesel. That was it, Miesel. Can you find him Jacob, and talk to him?'

'Aye. I'll get on it now.'

She raised her brows.

'Now? But the day is almost done.'

Jacob grinned.

'It never is. While your sort is enjoying yourselves at balls and parties and the like, the rest of us will be in the taverns dining on good ale and oysters!'

She laughed.

'Very well, then. But how will you find him?'

'Well, Sir Talbot was used to stable his cattle in the same mews as me lord, so that will be a start.'

CHAPTER THIRTEEN

Lucasta hurried back to her party to explain as best she could her long absence, while Jacob began his enquiries. These led him eventually to Cheapside. It was late and the clear day had given way to an equally clear night. Jacob was glad of his heavy surcoat to ward off the chilly air as he wandered through the darkening streets. There were few lights burning in the windows, although when he turned into Milk Street one bow window glowed with lamplight. Sounds of singing and raucous laughter escaped each time the door opened, evidence that the tavern was busy. Further along the street he saw another block of light, a shop window. As he drew near he could see a woman inside the shop, engaged in sweeping the floor. Her hair was hidden beneath a mob-cap but one or two red-gold locks had escaped and curled against her creamy cheeks. Her low neckline displayed an ample bosom and her sleeves were rolled up, exposing the soft white skin of her arms. When she stepped out to sweep her doorstep he observed that her kirtle was caught up out of the dirt, displaying her fine ankles to great advantage. Jacob stopped, admiring the view from the far side of the street, but at that moment two men came strolling by, arm in arm, commenting loudly upon the woman's charms as they reached the shop front. Jacob could not hear the words but their meaning was plain enough, and he could tell that the woman was affronted.

'Be off with you!' she cried, wielding her broom like a weapon before her.

The men laughed and moved on while the woman glared after them. Jacob grinned to himself.

'And you can begone, too,' snapped the woman, turning her attention to him. 'There's women a-plenty next door if that's what you're after.'

'No, no,' Jacob strolled towards her, touching his hat. 'I'm here on business.'

She curled her lip, a look of disbelief in her dark eyes.

'Well, go about your business, then.'

She propped the broom against the wall and reached for one of the window shutters.

'Here, let me do that.' Jacob stepped up and took the board from her. She watched him slot it into place over the window then silently handed him the next one.

'Thank you,' she muttered, when the final shutter was secured.

He looked up at the legend above the door.

'Mrs Sarah Jessop, cheesemonger.' He cocked one eyebrow at her. 'Would that be you, then?'

'And what if it is?'

'Then my business is with you, Mistress Jessop. Rather, it is with your tenant. I believe you have a gentleman lodging here, a Mr Miesel?' It seemed to him that she drew back a little.

'Oh? And what is he to you?'

'I've never yet met the man,' he answered mildly. 'I merely wants a word with him. Would he be within?'

'No, he isn't.' She picked up her broom and stepped back

into the doorway. He could see a narrow passage behind her leading to a flight of stairs, while an inner doorway to her right gave access to the cheese shop. 'You'll find him in the Raven.' She pointed across the road to the tavern. 'He takes his dinner there every night.'

He touched his hat again.

'Thank you, Mistress, I'm obliged to you.'

She rebuffed his smile with a suspicious glare, stepped back and slammed the door. Jacob stared at the closed door, grinning.

'As I said, ma'am, I'm obliged to you,' he repeated before retracing his steps and entering the tavern.

The air in the taproom was warm and fragrant with a mixture of ale, meat and onions. To one side there was a long table flanked by two benches. A number of men were gathered there to enjoy their dinner. Some wore livery and others were dressed in the black coat and knee-breeches favoured by the more personal servant. Jacob glanced along the row. There, near the far end of the table, was his quarry, a small neatly dressed man with close-set eyes and untidy, sandy-coloured hair that stuck out around his ears. He smiled inwardly; Miss Symonds had the right of it, describing the fellow as a weasel. He called for a jug of ale and a steak pie and took his seat at the long table. The conversation was free-flowing and noisy but not exclusive: within a few moments Jacob was joining in, explaining away his homespuns by saying he had been working for a country gentleman until the old man died and he been obliged to leave his livery behind.

'Aye, it's a poor do if yer gaffer snuffs it,' agreed his neighbour, shaking his head. 'The family wouldn't keep you on, then?'

'He didn't have no family,' returned Jacob. 'Place was shut

up. Can't imagine that happening here in London.'

'Oh, can't you?' grinned a liveried footman sitting oppo-site. 'Well, that's where you're wrong. The little shaver at the end of the table is in just such a pickle.'

'Lost 'is place, has he?' Jacob spoke casually, trying not to show too much interest.

'Not so much lost, 'ad it taken from him,' said Jacob's neighbour, coming back into the conversation. 'His master was murdered, and there's no one now to pay 'is wages.'

'Murdered!' Jacob gave a low whistle and the footman nodded.

'Aye, coming back to Lunnon he was, and our friend with him. You may think that a valet could live comfortable-like in his master's lodgings, until such times as things were sold up,' the footman continued, pre-empting Jacob's next question. 'But no. He packed his bags and quit the place as soon as maybe. Ain't that right, Dan?' He leaned forward to shout down the table, and Miesel raised his eyes from his dinner. 'It's true, ain't it, that you can't go back to Sir Talbot's lodgings?'

Miesel's pale eyes glanced around the table, resting briefly on Jacob, who schooled his features into a look of mild inter-est. He thought there was little chance that Miesel would recognize him: when their paths had crossed at Bromsgrove the valet had been too busy fawning upon his bullying master to spare a glance for a lowly groom. He kept his gaze upon Miesel as he gave his companions a sly smile.

'I was scared, you see: as witness to a murder and all, there's some might want to keep me quiet.'

Jacob leaned forward.

'You saw the murder?'

'Aye. I was there.'

One of the men reached for the blackjack of ale and refilled his mug.

'Tell us again what happened, Dan.'

'We'd not long been on the common when there comes a shot from behind the bushes. Sir Talbot takes out his pistol and begins to climb down from the curricle. "I'll hold 'em, Dan", he says. "Run and fetch help, man!" So I did, but by the time I got back he was lyin' dead on the road.'

'But they've got the culprit now,' chipped in the footman. 'A viscount, he is, and killed his man in cold blood.'

'You saw this viscount murder your master?' asked Jacob.

The valet's face took on a sly look.

'I saw a tall man in a greyish caped greatcoat and a beaver hat, and he had another man with him, a much shorter fellow. Slightly built. A lad, mebbe.'

'Kennington and his groom,' nodded another of his auditors. 'No doubt about it.'

Miesel shrugged.

'How can I say? I'm not going to perjure myself. It could have been Lord Kennington but I couldn't say for sure.' He took a long draught from his mug and dragged his hand across his mouth, adding with a sly grin, 'But like the magistrate said to me, how many tall gentlemen in light-coloured driving coats was crossing Hansford Common that day?'

'I thought you said the attackers were hiding,' said Jacob. 'If you ran off immediately, how did you see who was shooting at you?'

'They came out from hiding, as I made off,' said Miesel. 'And like I told the magistrate, if I saw *them*, 'tis very likely they saw me, and will want to silence me. "Don't you worry, my good man", he says to me, "we'll keep the villains clapped up. No harm will come to you". But what I says is, he'll have friends, this viscount, and they'll come to Sir Talbot's lodgings, looking for me, as sure as eggs.'

Miesel scowled into his mug and his neighbour clapped

him on the shoulder.

'No need to worry now, though, Dan. You're among friends here. We'll keep you safe to see justice is done.'

'Aye, justice,' nodded Jacob, raising his mug. 'I'll drink to that!'

CHAPTER FOURTEEN

An early morning airing gave Lucasta the opportunity for another meeting with Jacob Potts the next day, although with her pin-money spent she was obliged to buy her maid's silence by giving her one of her bonnets. Hannah was quite happy with this arrangement and even dropped back to a discreet distance while her mistress conducted her business. The maid considered Miss Symonds a very pleasant-spoken young lady, and when she saw the look of dismay on her mistress's face she surmised that the rough-looking man with the bad leg had brought her bad news. As they walked back to Sophia Street, Lucasta's distracted air seemed to confirm this view and when the young lady took herself off to her bedchamber, refusing breakfast, Hannah was seriously alarmed. She was debating whether she should break her silence and take Cook, who was her aunt, into her confidence, when she was ordered to carry a note to Miss Symonds. The message, whatever it was, worked like a charm upon the young lady: no sooner had she read its contents than she began to smile.

'Hannah,' she said, 'you had best fetch your bonnet and cloak again, for I need you to accompany me to see the Duchess of Filwood. *Now* we shall see some action!'

Lucasta went in search of her mother to ask her permission to call upon the duchess. She found Lady Symonds and Camilla still in the breakfast-room, where her announcement that she had received an invitation to visit Filwood House was received with dismay.

'Mama, you cannot allow it,' cried Camilla. 'We must keep our distance from this affair, you said so yourself.'

'I did, of course,' muttered Lady Symonds, carefully studying the note. 'However, it will not do to offend the Duchess of Filwood.'

'Especially when she has shown me so much kindness,' put in Lucasta.

'And her son, the duke, is still unmarried.'

'Really, Mama, how can that be important? Camilla is promised to Lord Kennington.'

'No, I am not,' said Camilla quickly. 'Nothing was formally agreed.'

'But much was implied!'

'That will do, Lucasta. We should all be thankful that no engagement has been announced. Once this sorry affair is settled then, of course, Camilla can resume her association with the viscount. Until then, well, since the duchess wishes to continue her acquaintance with you, Lucasta, I do not see it can do any harm, as long as you are discreet.'

'Then I may go, Mama?'

'I dare not refuse.'

Remembering her visit to Adam, Lucasta looked at her sister.

'The duchess will no doubt be seeing Lord Kennington, Camilla, do you have any message to pass to him?'

'No, nothing.' Camilla tossed her head. 'Pray do not look at me in that way, Lucasta. What would be said of me if it was known I was consorting with a criminal?'

'You are not very charitable, Sister.'

'There is no room here for charity,' cut in Lady Symonds. 'Camilla must maintain her reputation. And you must take care what you say to the duchess, Lucasta. You must do nothing to jeopardize our family. Perhaps I should come with you.'

Lucasta put up her hand, saying quickly, 'Her Grace has requested only me, Mama. We would not want to offend. . . .' She breathed sigh of relief when her mother accepted this and it was in a mood of optimism that she went off to collect her pelisse.

Lady Symonds ordered her carriage to take Lucasta the short distance to Filwood House. Leaving her maid to await her in the echoing hall, Lucasta followed the footman to the morning-room, where she was informed that her grace was expecting her. She entered with some trepidation, but as the door was closed upon them the duchess held out her hands, saying with her twinkling smile, 'I knew you would make a handsome young lady!'

With something like a sob Lucasta ran forward to clasp the beringed fingers.

'Your Grace, I am so glad you are here. I have been so wretched!'

'Well, I should think so, with Adam accused of murder and locked up in gaol!' She guided Lucasta to a sofa. 'Sit down, child. I had the story from Potts before he left me and I made sure all would be resolved by the time I came to Town. Instead I find everything in a sad pickle.'

'They – they will not g-grant him bail,' stammered Lucasta, blinking back the tears.

The duchess nodded.

'Aye, so I heard. However, I have set my own people to work on it and I expect them to deliver Adam here to me within the hour. No point in having family connections if one doesn't make use of 'em! So, tell me what has gone on here. No one knows of your part in this tangle?'

'No, ma'am, only my mother and sister, and they are very anxious that the story should not get out. Ad— I mean, Lord Kennington has forbidden me to tell anyone else; he says it will not help his case.'

'Quite right, too. It would only complicate matters. Best let the lawyers take care of it.'

'But you do not know the worst of it, ma'am. Potts went to see the dead man's valet last night, thinking to persuade him to talk again to the magistrates, to correct their assumption that Lord Kennington was the murderer, but he learned that it was the valet himself who has given my lord's description to the magistrate.'

'The devil he has!'

Miserably, Lucasta repeated everything Jacob Potts had told her while the duchess listened in frowning silence.

'Well it seems to me that this – this Miesel has his own reasons for putting the blame upon my godson.'

Lucasta nibbled on her finger, a tiny crease in her brow. 'It was Miesel who reported that a necklace had been stolen.' She looked up, wide-eyed, at the duchess. 'What if he stole the necklace for himself?'

'Then that would give him a very good reason for shuffling the blame onto someone else.' She bent her shrewd gaze upon Lucasta. 'You seem to know a great deal about this matter.'

'Potts came to find me yesterday: he was anxious for his master, and had no one else to call upon.'

'But that is not all, is it? I can see by your face that there is more.' With the duchess's piercing eyes fixed upon her, Lucasta felt the blood warming her cheeks. 'Well, child?'

'And' – the words were barely more than a whisper – 'and I went to Newgate, to see Lord Kennington.' She drew a breath. 'I was not recognized – I was heavily veiled, and no one knows of my visit, except Adam and now yourself.' She peeped up at her hostess and was relieved to see that the duchess was smiling.

'What a resourceful young lady you are.'

'They are saying such things of him in Town and I could not let him think he was friendless.'

The duchess patted her hands.

'You have a kind heart, Lucasta. Now we shall wait for Adam to arrive before we discuss what is to be done.'

It was almost an hour later when they heard sounds of an arrival. Lucasta jumped to her feet as the door opened and Lord Kennington walked in. When he saw Lucasta he paused, his brows rising in surprise. He made a small bow in her direction and strode across the room to the duchess.

'Godmama.' He kissed both her hands. 'I shall be eternally grateful to you for this. How did you secure my release?'

The duchess chuckled.

'Friends, my dear boy, friends in the highest places. I invited Miss Symonds to join us to decide how we are going to get you out of this scrape.'

'I am delighted to see you again, Miss Symonds.' The smile he directed towards her made Lucasta's heart flip over. 'And your family, they know that you are here?'

'They do, my lord.'

He continued to look at her: she saw the question in his eyes and it pained her that she could not answer it. At length he spoke again.

'Your sister is well, I hope?'

'Y-yes, sir. She is. She, um, she eagerly awaits news of your acquittal.'

'She does not wish to be associated with an accused murderer.'

The bitterness in his voice flayed her spirits. She could think of nothing to say. The duchess tapped his arm with her fan.

'Be sensible, Adam! An overt display of loyalty could ruin the chit.'

Lord Kennington's lip curled.

'Thank you for pointing that out, Your Grace.'

'Ungrateful dog! If you continue to look like that I shall wash my hands of you. Sit down, sir and let us decide what we are going to do.'

The viscount gave a short laugh.

'My apologies, Godmama, for my boorish manners.' He held out his hand to Lucasta. 'And to you, Miss Symonds. Will you not be seated?'

Having guided Lucasta to the sofa he sat down beside her and she could not quite crush the satisfaction she felt at his proximity.

'The first thing is to find Potts,' he said. 'My valet tells me he has gone into hiding to avoid being taken up.'

'Perhaps we should ask Miss Symonds where he may be found,' drawled the duchess.

Lord Kennington turned to look at her.

'You have seen Jacob?'

'He found *me*,' she murmured.

'Well, that is good news!' he exclaimed, grinning.

However, by the time she had related all her dealings with Jacob Potts and described his meeting with Miesel, none of them was smiling.

'It confirms my suspicions that Miesel is planning some game of his own. But he is clever: to identify me would condemn him, if I should prove my innocence. Much cleverer to give only a description: who is to say that it was not some chance attack by footpads? Witness our own encounter on the common. The key, I think, is the emerald necklace. If we find that, we shall find the murderer.'

'But how are we going to do that?' asked Lucasta.

The viscount's face darkened.

'I shall see Miesel and beat the truth out of him!'

'That you will not,' retorted the duchess. 'You must not do anything to make your own situation worse than it is; heaven knows you have already given everyone enough cause to suspect you.'

'I fear that was my fault, ma'am.' Lucasta was compelled to speak up. 'If I had not been with Lord Kennington he would not have been so anxious to quit the Pigeons at the earliest moment.'

'Oh yes I would!'

As Lucasta's eyes flew to his face he grinned at her.

'My bed was damnably uncomfortable, you know.'

The duchess waved an impatient hand.

'However that may be, you are going to remain here with me until we can bring this matter to a close.'

'Oh? And what does the duke say to that, having a felon in his house?'

'My son is in Yorkshire, so he can say nothing about it,' she returned with a twinkle. 'Although, I *have* left Giggs at Coombe Chase, and I have no doubt he has already written to Filwood to apprise him of this latest indiscretion. Now, I have summoned Gretton, for I knew you could not be persuaded to stay here without your valet: he is even now upstairs preparing your rooms for you.'

'And Potts?'

'I do not think we can guarantee his freedom, so for the moment perhaps it is best if he remains at large.'

The viscount sighed.

'I think you are right, ma'am. Jacob would detest Newgate.' He rose. 'If you will excuse me, I shall go and change. I am anxious to remove the stench of the prison cell from my person.'

Lucasta observed him from beneath her lashes: she thought he looked as immaculate as ever, only the grim set of his mouth and a slight shadowing under his eyes gave any hint of his ordeal. She stood up.

'I think I should go now.' She held out her hand to him. 'I am relieved that you are no longer in prison, my lord.'

He took her fingers and kissed them lightly.

'You must not worry, Lucasta. We shall soon resolve this matter.'

'I am sure we shall.' She gave him a faint smile then turned to make her curtsey to the duchess. 'I beg of you, ma'am, please keep me informed, and tell me if there is anything I can do – I want to help.'

'Bless you, child, I know that. If your mama will permit, I shall take you driving with me tomorrow, at which time I shall be able to tell you all that has happened. In fact – will you be at Lymington House this evening? Kennington shall introduce me to your mama and I will ask her myself if I can steal you away.'

'Godmama, you cannot expect me to go out with you tonight. I have no wish to be paraded before the *ton*—'

'Your wishes do not enter into this, Adam. You are innocent and we must make the world believe it!'

CHAPTER FIFTEEN

When she was informed that the Duchess of Filwood was coming to the assembly with the express intention of meeting her, Lady Symonds found herself in a dilemma. On the one hand she wanted to distance herself from the unsavoury events surrounding Lord Kennington: on the other, the duchess was influential in high circles and could prove very useful in securing a brilliant alliance for Camilla, something that might be necessary if the viscount should be found guilty. Therefore, she girded herself in her finest straw-coloured lustring and sallied forth to do her duty.

Very few of the gowns ordered for Lucasta had arrived and she had to decide between the altered tawny silk gown of her mother's, or a green sacque-back robe over embroidered cream petticoats. She chose the green. It was not her favourite, but her mama had assured her when she purchased it that the colour accentuated her flawless skin and she was honest enough to admit that she wanted to look her best for Lord Kennington. However, as she joined her mother and sister in the entrance hall of Lymington House she glanced at herself critically in one of the large, gilt-framed mirrors and sighed. What did it matter what she wore when Camilla was looking radiant in celestial blue satin and gauze?

The ballroom was already crowded when Lady Symonds and her daughters arrived but they were by no means the last and, as the rooms filled, so the laughter and chattering grew ever louder, which made the sudden lull all the more dramatic when the Duchess of Filwood arrived with Lord Kennington. Lucasta wanted to laugh aloud at the shocked faces around her. The duchess sailed in on the viscount's arm, her hair dressed high in an elaborate coiffure and ornamented with nodding ostrich plumes. At her side was the viscount, magnificent in black velvet trimmed with gold and enlivened at the throat and wrists by a froth of snow-white lace. She had to admire him: in the momentary silence he raised his quizzing glass and looked around with just a touch of hauteur on his lean, handsome features. Gradually the noise began again, conversations were taken up, groups moved off to the ballroom and several people hurried forward to greet the duchess. All was as it should be.

It was not long before Lord Kennington escorted the duchess across to Lady Symonds. He performed the introductions smoothly. The duchess smiled, exchanged a few words with Lady Symonds then beckoned Camilla to come forward.

'Well, Kennington, you did not lie when you told me Miss Camilla was a beauty. No need to colour up, my dear: you will find I always speak my mind. How are you enjoying your first season?'

'Very much, if it please Your Grace.' Camilla curtseyed and modestly lowered her eyes.

'Hmm. I am sure you never lack for partners.'

'Indeed, Your Grace, everyone has been most kind,' put in

Lady Symonds. 'When we first arrived in Town we had but a few acquaintances but that is all changed now. There are so many invitations we are rarely at home, and the season proper has not yet begun.'

The duchess agreed, complimented Lady Symonds upon her handsome daughters and prepared to move away, promising to call for Miss Symonds in her carriage at the fashionable hour the following day. Lucasta was still reeling in admiration at the duchess's tactics when she heard the viscount asking Camilla to stand up with him. Camilla blushed and plied her fan.

'I am very sorry – I did not expect – that is, I am engaged for every – I mean, I do have one country dance later, if you should be free?'

Lucasta's jaw clenched in anger. She saw the cold, closed look descend upon the viscount's face as he bowed and turned away. She curled her hands around the sticks of her closed fan, her nails digging into the palms: Camilla's behaviour had roused her anger, but added to that was disappointment that Adam had not asked her to dance with him. It was very lowering to discover that she would gladly have accepted second best.

Lord Kennington did not approach them again until he came to claim his country dance, but before he led Camilla away he turned to Lucasta.

'Miss Symonds, my godmother begs for the pleasure of your company at supper.'

'I would be delighted, my lord,' she replied quickly, without reference to her mother, standing cold and silent beside her.

He bowed.

'Then I hope you will permit me to escort you to her, when this dance is ended.'

'You are determined to flout me,' hissed Lady Symonds, as Lord Kennington moved off.

'I am merely trying to make up for your cold manner, ma'am,' flashed Lucasta. 'It would not be so bad if you had not courted his favour so assiduously at Oaklands.'

She saw the angry flush mounting her mother's cheeks. Lady Symonds hunched her shoulder and turned away, leaving Lucasta alone to watch the dancing. She found little to amuse her: Camilla was clearly uncomfortable in the viscount's company, avoiding his glance and barely speaking a word when the dance brought them together. Such was her dismay that Lucasta felt obliged to comment as Lord Kennington led her off to the supper room.

'You must forgive my sister, sir. When we arrived tonight she was besieged by gentlemen, begging her to dance with them.'

'You need not apologize: I understand perfectly.'

Lucasta winced at his cold tone.

'She is very young, my lord. I fear the adulation she has received since coming to Town has gone to her head.' When he did not reply she added quietly, 'She truly was engaged for every dance, you know.'

He relaxed slightly and gave her a wry smile.

'And you have not been far behind her: you, too, have been on the dance floor most of the evening.'

'Yes, it is very fortunate that the gentlemen who fail to secure my sister feel obliged to take me instead.'

'You are too hard on yourself, Miss Symonds; some may be dazzled initially by your sister's beauty, but it should not take a discerning man very long to realize your worth.'

She gave a little gasp.

'Oh, pray do not think I was looking for a compliment, my lord.'

He pressed her fingers, lying snug upon his velvet sleeve. 'I would never think that of you, Lucasta.'

She was inordinately pleased at his words and as they reached the duchess's table her warm greeting added even more to her pleasure although her spirits faltered a little when she saw Camilla enter the room upon the arm of a fashionable young gentleman. She quickly looked away and began to chatter, hoping that her companions would not notice Camilla's arrival but the viscount had already seen her.

'Your sister does not lack for admirers, Miss Symonds. She is much more comfortable with that young buck than with such a disreputable person as myself.'

'Pray do not be angry with her, sir.'

'No indeed, Adam,' said the duchess. 'Miss Camilla is not yet sure of her place in society. Allow her a little time to find her feet, my boy.'

'She knows you are innocent of the charges against you,' said Lucasta in a low voice. He looked across the table at her, a faint cynical twist to his smile that wrenched at her heart and made her add in a fierce undervoice, 'We shall find the real killers, Adam. We shall find them, then everyone will know that you are innocent!'

CHAPTER SIXTEEN

Lucasta was accompanying Lord Kennington and the duchess out of the supper room when an elderly gentleman entered. Upon seeing them he stopped, effectively blocking the doorway.

'Oh lord,' muttered the viscount. 'General Bradfield, Sir Talbot's uncle.'

'Hush now,' replied the duchess quietly. She continued towards the door. 'Good evening, Nicholas.'

The old man did not bow, but glared at them from beneath shaggy brows. Despite his age his bearing was very upright and he cut an impressive figure as he stood before them.

'So, Tabitha, it has come this, that your godson has seen fit to despatch my nephew.'

'Pray do not talk such nonsense, Nicholas. We both know Kennington is no murderer.'

'Well, we shall see, we shall see.'

The duchess tapped her cane on the floor.

'You are in the way, Nicholas. Pray stand aside, sir!'

The general looked around and with a smothered oath he moved away from the door, shaking his stick at the interested crowd, that had gathered behind him. When the crowd had dispersed, he fixed his fierce gaze upon the viscount.

'Where, sir, are the Bradfield emeralds?'

'I really have no idea. My rooms and my . . . person have been searched, so you must be aware that I do not have them.'

Lucasta's hand was on Adam's arm, and instinctively her grip tightened as she heard the anger in his voice.

'Well, we shall know soon enough,' barked the general. 'I have set my own men on to it, and I've offered a reward of a hundred guineas for information – what do you think of that?'

'I hope it will help us to find the real culprits,' replied the duchess.

'Oh, you may be sure it will. I've put the word about pretty widely – all the jewellers in London will be on their guard and I have contacts in the rookeries, too: they will not be able to sell a single gem without word getting back to me.'

'One would think, General,' mused the duchess, 'that you are more concerned with recovering the emeralds than finding your nephew's killer.'

'What's that?' Beneath its whiskers the old man's face grew red. 'Well, of course I want to find Talbot's murderer! Not that I was surprised when I heard the news. Talbot was always – his manner of living – well, never mind that!' He glared at the viscount again. 'If you say you didn't do it, Kennington, then I want to believe you, but it all comes down to the evidence, my boy, the evidence.'

With a curt nod he strode away, snarling at anyone who chanced in his way.

Lucasta glanced around.

'Dear ma'am,' she murmured, aghast, 'so many people were listening! It will be all over Town tomorrow.'

'Perfect,' smiled the duchess. 'I may think Nicholas an old fool, but the fact that he is inclined to believe Adam innocent will weigh with many. Now, my dear, we must return you to your mama before she thinks you have been thoroughly corrupted.'

When the duchess's carriage pulled up in Sophia Street the following afternoon Lucasta hurried out, full of optimism. The duchess was wrapped up in velvet and furs against the chill spring air and she looked concerned as Lucasta was handed up.

'My dear, do you have nothing warmer to put on? Your pelisse looks dreadfully thin for an open carriage.'

'It is finest English wool, Your Grace and I have a warm gown beneath it.'

'Well you shall have a rug across your knees.' She signalled to the footman to perform this service. 'It would, of course, be much warmer to be in a closed carriage but we must see and be seen in Hyde Park at the fashionable hour.'

'It would also be more private,' observed Lucasta, glancing at the liveried back of the coachman.

'It would, of course, although I pay my people very well and in return I demand their total discretion. Besides, I have nothing to say that cannot be overheard.' She sighed. 'Unfortunately, Miss Symonds, there is very little to tell you. My lawyer informs me that he has been expressly warned not to talk to the valet. It seems the man fears that my godson will try to intimidate him.'

'But that is monstrous!'

'Of course it is, but there is nothing to be done. Just as there is nothing to be done about the fellow who is following us.'

Lucasta twisted round and observed a solitary rider trotting along behind them.

'He is in General Bradfield's pay,' explained the duchess.

'A man has also been assigned to follow Kennington. Oh, you need not look so dismayed, my dear, one grows accustomed. However, it does restrict Adam: he wanted to go back to Hansford Common to find the footpads who accosted you, but now that is impossible. I think I must employ a thief-taker of my own.'

'Do you think the general will have me followed too?' asked Lucasta, a thoughtful crease on her brow.

'Lord, I hope not! If he means to set a fellow on every one of my acquaintance, poor Nicholas will be a pauper by the end of the week.' She broke off as they turned into Rotten Row. There were dozens of carriages to be seen and Lucasta was surprised when the duchess observed that it was exceedingly quiet. 'Of course, it is not yet April: at the height of the season one is reduced to a snail's pace. Oh – look, there are Lady Spencer and her daughters. Pull up, Shankster, I will speak with the countess.'

'Well, Lucasta, I hope you enjoyed your drive with the duchess?'

'Yes, Mama, I did, thank you.'

Unusually, Lady Symonds was dining at home with her daughters and there was nothing to distract her from Lucasta's inconsiderate behaviour.

'I should very much like to drive in Hyde Park,' remarked Camilla, helping herself to buttered parsnips. 'Everyone of fashion does so.'

'Indeed they do,' agreed Lucasta. 'In one short drive we saw the Duchess of Devonshire with her mama and her sister, Lady Bessborough. And when we drove along Piccadilly, the Duke of Queensberry was just stepping out of his house.'

Lady Symonds's knife clattered on to her plate.

'Merciful heavens, did the duchess introduce you to all of them?'

'Yes,' replied Lucasta, all wide-eyed innocence. 'Her grace is acquainted with everyone.'

'You delight in vexing me,' retorted her mama, tight-lipped. 'Is it not enough that you consort with murderers, you must also ally yourself with the Devonshire set?'

'And March,' murmured Lucasta. 'The Duke of Queensberry was most friendly.'

'Lucasta,' breathed Camilla, shocked, 'even *I* know better than to encourage that rake.'

'So too do I,' said Lucasta, a laugh trembling in her voice, 'But I could not forbear to tease you both a little. I am very sorry,' she ended contritely.

'But the Devonshires,' sighed Camilla, 'If we were to become part of that set—'

'We should need a great deal more money to spend,' retorted Lady Symonds. 'Not but what a little more investment might not pay dividends, for it would put Camilla into the way of many more eligible suitors. And you too, Lucasta.'

'Thank you, Mama, but I have no wish to join you in this. I am already going abroad a great deal more than I would wish.'

'You would be best to get yourself a husband and have done with it.' put in Camilla. 'It is plain from Papa's letter that he does not want you at home.'

Lucasta looked up. 'What is this?'

Lady Symonds dabbed at her lips with her napkin.

'I received a letter today, from Oaklands. It arrived while you were out.'

'Papa says you completely misunderstood the situation,' said Camilla. 'Squire Woodcote did intend to propose but there was not the least idea of coercion.'

Lucasta stared at her mother.

'And you believe that?'

Lady Symonds looked uncomfortable.

'You would not have me accuse your father of telling lies, I am sure.'

Lucasta felt slightly sick.

'You would not send me back, Mama.'

'No, no, of course not. Although your father assures me Squire Woodcote is now looking elsewhere for a bride. But I shall write again to your papa and tell him that now you are here I had as well keep you with me. And if we can find you a husband, all the better.'

'You could come with us to Almack's,' suggested Camilla. 'We would wait for you, if you wanted to change your gown.'

But on this point Lucasta was adamant and she saw her mother and sister off before retiring to the drawing-room with her book. She had visited the assembly rooms last year during her own short come-out and had not enjoyed it. She had felt very much like a prize sow dragged out for inspection – no wonder Almack's was known as the Marriage Mart. But there was another reason why she did not venture out that evening: she was expecting a visit from Jacob Potts.

CHAPTER SEVENTEEN

At precisely 11.30 she made her way downstairs to the domestic offices of the house, her darkest pelisse pulled around her. She tiptoed past the housekeeper's sitting-room and let herself out through the cold, damp scullery. The house Lady Symonds had hired for the season was one of a terrace of town houses, each with a small yard at the back enclosed by a wall, too high to see over but easily scaled by an agile man and hopefully, thought Lucasta, by a man recovering from a leg wound. She hovered in the shadows of the house and soon saw a figure scrambling over the wall. She stepped forward.

'Jacob?'

'Aye, miss, it's me. What news is there?'

Briefly she told him of her meeting with the duchess and as she finished he muttered an oath, slamming his fist into his palm.

'Beggin' your pardon, miss, but it fair irks me to think o' that rogue cutting a sham!'

'You do not think he could be innocent, that it really was footpads? After all, we were accosted on the same common only a few hours earlier.'

'Aye, but that was on t'other side of the common. I grant

you they could have struck again, but I don't see them travelling that far. And that doesn't explain Miesel's describing my lord so perfectly, now, does it? Besides, having nothing better to do, I've been keeping an eye on Miesel and he seems to have a taste for low company. Keeps taking himself off to the seedy parts of the town where he visits the pop-shops.'

'What are they?'

'Pawnbrokers, miss. But not your regular brokers: I don't reckon the ones Miesel visits pay their dues to the workhouses. And Sarah – Mrs Jessop, that is – his landlady, she don't like him neither.'

'But that is not proof that he is a villain,' replied Lucasta.

'No. If we could prove he had the emeralds that would be something.'

'Perhaps we can,' she said slowly. 'He goes out a great deal, does he? What if we were to search his lodgings?'

Jacob Potts shook his head.

'Very risky: he could return at any moment, then where would we be? Then there's Mrs Jessop: she's in her shop all day and would be bound to notice.'

'Not necessarily. You could distract her, Jacob, and you could keep a lookout for Miesel at the same time while I search his room.'

'No!' Potts' explosive whisper sent a prowling tomcat leaping away over the wall. 'There's no question of you doing such a thing, miss. Only think!'

'I *am* thinking. With Adam and her grace being watched there is no one else to help.'

It took her some considerable time to persuade Jacob to go along with her plan and it was only when he realized that she was prepared to attempt it alone that he agreed to help.

'Good. We must waste no time, Jacob. Have a carriage

waiting at the end of the lane here as soon as it is dark tomorrow night.'

It was not difficult for Lucasta to feign a headache the following day and her mama was easily persuaded to leave her at home when she took Camilla out to be the belle of another fashionable ball. Lucasta shut herself in her room with instructions she was not to be disturbed and, as dusk was falling, she pulled out the boy's clothes she had worn on her journey to London, ready for her nocturnal adventure.

The noisy, narrow streets off Cheapside were a little daunting after the wide thoroughfares of the more fashionable part of town and Lucasta was glad she was not alone. Jacob Potts led her past crowded taverns and alehouses until they reached the bright windows of the cheesemonger. She could see a woman inside the lighted shop, piling up the large, muslin-wrapped cheeses. Lucasta observed with approval the clean windows and freshly scrubbed doorstep.

'Mistress Jessop appears to be a proud housewife,' she murmured, glancing up at Jacob. Something in his look made her add, 'It's enough to give a man a liking for fine cheese.'

She smiled inwardly when he looked a little self-conscious, but her momentary good humour was replaced with anxiety when she thought of what must come next.

'Well, Jacob, we had better get on.'

'Aye, miss. There's no light in the upstairs window so I'm pretty sure Miesel's gone out.

Lucasta breathed out slowly, trying to calm her nerves. She swallowed hard.

'Very well then, if you go in and distract her, I will slip up the stairs.'

Potts hesitated.

'I don't like it, miss, deceiving a good woman like this.'

'Perhaps you would prefer to tell her the truth.'

'Well, that I would, miss, and that's a fact, but I don't suppose she could agree to it.'

'Of course she could not. Come, Jacob, she's alone now: let us get it over with.'

They crossed the street, Lucasta hanging back in the shadows as Jacob stepped over the threshold and hesitated at the inner doorway.

'Oh, so it's you come back again. Don't tell me you've eaten a whole pound o' cheese already!'

'I've never known a mite with such a good range o' cheeses as you have here, mistress. . . .'

As Mistress Jessop turned her back to the door Lucasta slipped inside and up the darkened staircase. The pungent smell from the shop followed her as she crept up the stairs and she was glad when the clatter of a passing wagon helped to cover the slight thud of her boots on the wooden treads. When she reached the top she paused, listening, but the only sound was the soft rumble of voices from the shop below. She felt in her pocket for the tinderbox and with shaking fingers managed to light the small stub of candle she had brought with her. There was a sudden moment of panic at the thought that the rooms might be locked, but the candlelight showed her three plain panelled doors. Jacob had told her that Miesel was renting the room at the front of the house, over the shop. There was no light showing beneath the door, and when Lucasta held her breath to listen she could hear no noise other than the erratic thudding of her own heart. Wiping her sweating palm against her jacket, she reached out and tried the handle.

The door opened with barely a creak and she slipped into

the room. Everything was neat and orderly, the narrow bed made up and curtains pulled across the window. The odour of cheese permeated the room, where it mixed with the smell of soap and soot and hair oil. If it had not been for the clothes folded neatly over the chair and the brush and comb lying amongst an assortment of bottles on top of a chest of drawers, she would have thought it unoccupied. Carefully putting down the candle she began to look through the drawers. Her hands were shaking and she felt quite sick, sure that at any moment she would be discovered. Only her determination to prove Adam's innocence kept her from running away. The top drawer contained only clothes, neatly folded, but in the second she found a silver-backed brush and matching comb. Closer inspection showed the silver to be engraved with the initials TB. Talbot Bradfield. Was it normal, she wondered, for a servant to be given such things when his master died, or had Miesel helped himself to these valuable objects? Buried further down was an enamelled card case, various tie pins and a gold pocket watch. She guessed these were the goods he was pawning and it explained the use of illicit brokers – Miesel would not want it known that he was passing on his dead master's goods. She shivered, carefully placed everything back as she had found it and continued her search.

The drawers yielded nothing other than a few more trinkets and she turned her attention to the trunk at the end of the bed. A sudden burst of laughter from the shop below reminded her that Jacob was waiting for her. She must hurry; it would look suspicious if he was to tarry too long. Or would it? The thought became a little bubble of nervous laughter to mix with the fear inside her. It seemed there was a budding friendship between Jacob and the widow Jessop. She only hoped their exploits this evening would not jeopardize it. Swiftly she opened the trunk and searched through the contents, checking coat pockets, feeling between folds of material. There was nothing. Carefully she replaced the clothes and closed the trunk. She looked in desperation around the little room. She had no time to move the furniture, nor could she make any noise without risking detection.

In a final, desperate bid she took the stub of candle and knelt down to look under the bed. The flickering light showed her that there was nothing there except the chamber pot. She noticed an extended shadow where one of the floorboards was not quite flat. She reached out and pressed the corner: it felt loose. Carefully she moved the chamber pot to one side and closed her trembling fingers around the edge of the board. It came away surprisingly easily, for it was a very short length, recently cut. Her heart began to beat so hard she could not breathe. Fighting down very rational fears of mice and spiders lurking in dark places she reached into the space beneath the boards and almost immediately her fingers closed around a leather pouch. She pulled it out and sat back, hardly daring to believe what she had done. Untying the strings of the pouch, she tipped it up and onto her outstretched palm slithered a glittering emerald necklace.

CHAPTER EIGHTEEN

'. . . I sell cheeses from all over the country, many brought in by sea. Those truckles came in today from the north country.' Sarah Jessop indicated the large cheeses stacked on the counter. Jacob nodded, impressed. He was leaning against the wall in the far corner of the room so that Sarah had her back turned to the door as she talked to him.

'And your husband was a cheesemonger too?'

'He didn't start as a mite. He was a cheese maker. Aye, and he was good, too, God rest his soul. Finest in Hampshire, until he decided to come to London and open his own shop. His family still make cheese there, you know, and send it up for me to sell.'

'Have you never thought of going back to Hampshire then?'

Her ready laugh burst forth again. Jacob admired the smooth line of her throat as she tilted her head back. She regarded him with a merry twinkle in her eyes.

'What, go back to live with the family and lose my independence? Why ever should I want to do that?'

'Oh, I don't know. It must be hard, without a husband, running a business.'

'Aye it is, but I can buy in labour when I need it: I don't need to marry a man for that.'

From the corner of his eye Jacob glimpsed a slight figure slipping out of the door. Miss Symonds was done. He pushed himself upright and was aware of a slight feeling of regret mingled with his relief that the job was over. He picked up the package from the counter.

'I look forward to having a taste o' this for me supper. Thank you again, Mistress Jessop. Perhaps I'll come back and try all your cheeses.'

Her laughing eyes rested on him for a long moment, appraising him.

'Aye,' she said, 'mayhap you will.'

Jacob doffed his cap and limped out, looking neither right nor left until he came to the corner of the street, where Miss Symonds was waiting for him, hands stuffed into the pockets of her ill-fitting jacket and her muffler wound around her face.

'I expected you to follow me immediately, Jacob. What kept you?'

'I had to finish me conversation with Mistress Jessop. Wouldn't do to make her suspicious.' He smiled. And it had not been an onerous task to be pleasant to the widow. 'Well, did you find the necklace?'

Even in the dim lamplight he could see the excitement shining in her eyes.

'Yes, it was hidden in a bag under the floor.'

She turned to walk beside him.

'Good. Let us find a cab and you can show me.'

'I haven't got it.'

Jacob stopped.

'What?'

'I left the necklace in Miesel's room.' She gripped his arm.

'How would it look if we took it and said where we had found it? Miesel could deny it and say we were trying to put the blame on him.'

'So what do you think to do now? If we tell anyone where it is Miesel is just as likely to say we put it there!'

'Yes,' she said, nodding vigorously. 'That is why we have to be even cleverer than Miesel. We must set a trap for him.'

'Oh? And just how do we do that?'

She did not appear to notice his sarcasm but continued to walk beside him, shoulders hunched and a frowning look upon her face.

'Just at present I do not know, but once I have spoken to Lord Kennington—'

'Heaven and earth, you ain't going to tell 'im we searched Miesel's rooms?'

'But of course!'

'Then you don't tell 'im I was helping you! If his lordship knew I had let you put yourself in so much danger—'

'Well, he cannot do anything to you since he does not know where you are,' reasoned Lucasta.

He gave a groan.

'The sooner I get you home the better, miss.'

'Yes, I think so, too,' came the sunny reply. 'The only thing is, well, would you mind coming to the back of the house with me? You see, I used an upturned pail to get over the wall, and I do not think I can get back in without help.'

'It must be near midnight,' whispered Lucasta, as they walked along the alley at the rear of Sophia Street.

'I hope you are keeping count of these houses,' grumbled Jacob. 'There's no telling which one is which from this side.'

'Oh, you need not worry, I left a lamp burning in my bedroom window – look, there it is.' She hurried on a few more paces and stopped. 'This is where I climbed over. Help me up, Jacob—'

'Oh no, you don't!'

Lucasta gave a little scream as the strange voice boomed out of the darkness.

'What the— Who's there?' demanded Jacob, moving closer to Lucasta.

'More to the point, who have we here?' demanded the voice and Lucasta gave another little cry as a heavy hand fell on her shoulder.

'What in— Get your hands off me!' cried Jacob, struggling with the dark figure.

'Oh ho, don't you try to resist arrest, my man. I'm taking you back to Bow Street.'

'A Runner!' exclaimed Lucasta. 'But – but you cannot arrest us! We have done nothing wrong.'

'That's humbug, when I've seen you with me own eyes!'

'You couldn't have done!' exclaimed Jacob wrathfully.

'That's where you are wrong. I've been following you from Cheapside where I saw *you*, me lad, cutting a sham with the widow lady while your young accomplice here did a spot o' breaking and entering.'

'That's not true because there was nothing to break,' retorted Lucasta, wriggling again to try to shake off the restraining hand. 'The doors were not locked.'

'Now don't you try to get clever with me, my lad. I'm an officer of the law.'

Lucasta stopped struggling.

'Who set you on?' she demanded.

'That, my lad, is none of your—'

'Was it the Duchess of Filwood?' asked Lucasta, ignoring him. 'She said she would appoint someone. You may as well tell us, for it cannot be a secret.'

'As a matter of fact, it was on her grace's orders—'

'I knew it!' exclaimed Lucasta, clapping her hands. 'So you can release us now, sir, for you are on our side.' The heavy hand on her shoulder did not lift.

'The law,' said the voice impressively, 'does not take sides.'

Lucasta gave a sigh of exasperation. 'I am Miss Symonds and well acquainted with her grace – she may even have told you about me. And this is Lord Kennington's groom.'

'Ah. Now I recall there *was* some mention of a groom.'

At last the grip on her shoulder relaxed, but rather than showing gratitude, she demanded angrily, 'So why are you here with us, instead of watching the true culprit?'

'Well, miss, maybe that's because I ain't yet sure who is the real culprit. You see, I was down in Cheapside, keeping an eye on a certain Mr Miesel when I sees you two coming to his abode and acting most suspicious. So when you leaves, I follows you, see and finds you acting even more suspicious here.'

'But I live here,' explained Lucasta.

'Then why don't you go in by the front door, like any Christian lady?'

'Well – well, I do not want anyone to see me dressed like this.'

'And there's another question.' The voice was beginning to deepen again. 'What is a young lady doing dressed in those togs?'

'I think this is going to be a long story,' put in Jacob. 'Do you think we could find somewhere else to discuss this?'

'Aye,' growled the voice. 'I think I had best take you both to Bow Street.'

'No, I have a much better idea,' said Lucasta, thinking quickly. 'We should all go inside. I could order you a hot drink, or a jug of ale,' she added persuasively.

'And just how are we to get in, miss?'

'Why over the wall, of course.'

The shadowy figure drew itself up to an impressive height.

'It would not be conducive with my calling for me to be climbing over walls.'

'Well, how would it be if I climbed over the wall and you and Jacob could call at the front door? By the time you have been shown in I will have changed into a gown and be fit to receive you. What do you say?'

'That sounds like a very good plan,' said Jacob, whose injured thigh was beginning to ache.

The voice was not too sure.

'How do I know you will not run away again?'

'Because I *live* here,' she said patiently. 'Besides, even if I did run away you would still have Mr Potts, now, wouldn't you?'

'No.' The voice was suddenly decisive. 'I don't think I can do that, miss. I have only your word that you lives here: I might be helping you to commit a felony.'

She bit back a sharp retort.

'Very well,' she said, 'we must all go to Filwood House!'

CHAPTER NINETEEN

Thus it was that at some few minutes to midnight, the duchess's astonished butler opened the door to find three strange men on the doorstep, demanding entrance. He was about to say that her grace was not at home when the largest of the men stepped forward.

'If you would be so good as to tell her grace that Mr Loughton is here to see her – from Bow Street.'

Oozing disapproval, the butler ushered them into the library and bade them wait there while he informed his mistress of their arrival. A footman was lighting candles around the room and Lucasta kept to the shadows until he reluctantly withdrew, then she turned to take her first good look at a Bow Street Runner.

He was a large man dressed unobtrusively in a brown jacket and breeches with a heavy surcoat over all and a shallow-crowned beaver atop his own unpowdered hair. His craggy face was set in sober lines but she thought she detected a gleam of humour in his sharp eyes. A long-case clock in one corner chimed the hour.

'Midnight,' remarked Mr Loughton. 'I do hope her ladyship ain't one for early nights.'

'Fortunately for you, Mr Loughton, I am not!'

They all turned as the Duchess of Filwood came into the room, followed closely by Lord Kennington.

From her shadowy corner Lucasta watched as the viscount's eyes swept around the room. For a moment he held her gaze, his face impassive, before moving on. He saw his groom and strode across to grip his hand.

'Well, Potts, so we have found you at last! How is the leg?'

'Not too bad, sir, if I am allowed to rest it now and then.'

'Then let us all sit down,' said the duchess. 'Perhaps someone will explain to me just what is the meaning of this invasion.'

'Mr Loughton wanted to arrest us,' said Lucasta, taking off her hat and shaking out her hair. 'For acting suspiciously.'

The duchess's lips twitched.

'Good heavens.'

'Aye, Your Grace.' Mr Loughton stepped forward. 'This – um – this *young person* says she is a friend of yours, ma'am, and this – er – gentleman claims to be his lordship's groom.'

'He was going to take us to Bow Street,' explained Lucasta, 'so I suggested we should come here instead. It is very late, and I am sorry, but I could not think what else to do. I thought you could vouch for us, Your Grace.'

'Well *I* can vouch for Potts,' put in the viscount, 'if not the – er – young person.'

Lucasta threw him a fulminating glance and the duchess shook her head at him.

'Pray do not be provoking, Kennington. Miss Symonds is indeed known to me, Mr Loughton, although why she is dressed in that strange garb I am at a loss to understand.'

'I went with Mr Potts to Miesel's lodgings,' said Lucasta. 'I had to leave the house without being seen, which meant climbing over the back wall and I could not possibly do that in a gown.'

'No. I quite see that,' murmured the duchess, her eyes twinkling.

'I knew you would understand, Your Grace. We were looking for any clue that would help Lord Kennington.'

'And did you find anything?'

'As a matter of fact, Your Grace—' Potts began, but Lucasta interrupted him.

'No. We found nothing.' She cast what she hoped was an appealing look at the Runner. 'So, no harm done?'

He wagged an admonishing finger at her.

'Well, not this time, but if you wants to stay out of trouble, miss, I suggest you leave this investigation to me.'

'Yes, indeed you must, my dear,' her grace agreed. 'It is Loughton's job to prove my godson's innocence.'

The Runner coughed.

'In actual fact, ma'am, my job is to find a certain emerald necklace and to find Sir Talbot Bradfield's murderer or murderers, whoever they may be.'

The duchess put up her brows.

'Indeed? Well the reward I have put up depends upon Kennington being found *not* guilty.'

Mr Loughton looked apologetic.

'Forgive me, Your Grace, but there is still General Bradfield's reward of one hundred guineas, whosoever is found guilty.'

The viscount laughed.

'It seems you cannot lose, then, Mr Loughton.'

A reluctant grin creased the Runner's face.

'Indeed I cannot, my lord, although I don't mind saying I am hoping the guilty party won't turn out to be your lordship.'

'I am very glad to hear you say that, Mr Loughton,' remarked the duchess, 'but perhaps I should tell you that while you have been chasing around London after my young friend here, there has been a development.'

'Oh, Your Grace? And how came you to know about it so soon?'

'Because I am paying a great deal of money for the services of you and your colleagues,' she retorted.

'But what is this ... development, ma'am?' Lucasta stepped forward eagerly. 'Has a witness come forward? Is Lord Kennington cleared?'

'No.'

Lucasta could not read the strange look that accompanied this monosyllable. After a moment the duchess said slowly, 'They have found young Mr Smith.'

CHAPTER TWENTY

Lucasta stared.

'But that is impossible!'

'Yes, it would seem so,' remarked Lord Kennington. Especially when we all thought he was going into the north country, but we have had word that he was arrested at Bromsgrove and has been brought to Newgate.'

'But it cannot – I mean—' She stopped. 'How can they be sure it is the same man?'

The duchess flicked open her fan and waved it gently.

'Apparently, he answers the description given by the landlord at the Pigeons.'

'Well, well, here's good news indeed!' cried Mr Loughton, rubbing his large hands together. 'Perhaps now we shall have some answers.'

'I would certainly like to talk to Mr Smith,' murmured the viscount.

Mr Loughton drew himself up to his full and impressive height.

'Now that, my lord, is quite out of the question, seeing as

how you and Mr Smith could be accomplices in this crime. I must give you a word of warning, sir, that you is not to make any attempt to see the prisoner. You have been bailed, sir, but you could be clapped up again very easily, you know.'

'Thank you, Mr Loughton, for that timely reminder.' Lord Kennington bowed. 'Now, may I suggest that you return to your duties?'

'Aye, I think I had best look in at Bow Street to find out the latest news.' The Runner rubbed his chin. 'I seem to recall that the Justice of the Peace wants to question Mr Potts. . . .'

'Yes, yes, but surely he will not wish to do so at this time of night,' put in the duchess. 'I would suggest, Mr Loughton, that you leave Mr Potts in my care. The magistrate may question him whenever he pleases.'

'Thank you, Your Grace. That I will.'

'Good. And before you go, Mr Loughton, perhaps you would like some refreshment after all your trouble,' The duchess waved one regal hand. 'Show him out, Kennington, and tell my people to take him to the buttery for some bread and ale.'

The Runner made a low bow.

'Well, that is very generous of you, ma'am, very generous indeed. A little drop o' something would set me up nicely.'

They watched in silence as the viscount accompanied Mr Loughton out of the room. As the door closed behind them Jacob gave a noisy sigh of relief.

'Well that was a close one! I was sure he would take me off to the lock-up.'

'Now that you have been found, Potts, I think we must keep you here,' said the duchess. 'My lawyers shall begin working on it in the morning. I see no need for you to be locked up.'

'Good God no,' added the viscount, coming back into the room. 'I have done without your services long enough, Jacob; it would be most inconvenient if they were to put you in gaol.'

Potts grinned. Lucasta, frowning, exclaimed, 'But what of this Mr Smith they have arrested? What are we going to do about him?'

'The report we received says he was caught trying to sell a snuff-box of Sir Talbot's,' said the viscount. 'It appears General Bradfield posted notices everywhere, including Hansford Common and someone was sharp-eyed enough to spot young – er – Mr Smith.'

'But we know he cannot be – I mean—'

'We certainly need to know how he fits into this tangle,' agreed the duchess. 'We need to talk to him. Lucasta, my dear, I think you must go to Newgate again.'

'Me?' squeaked Lucasta.

'No!' said the viscount explosively. 'It is far too dangerous. I am surprised you can even suggest it, ma'am.'

The duchess did not look at all put out.

'*You* are obliged to remain here, Adam, and *I* cannot go, I am far too conspicuous, but there is no reason why Lucasta should not go to the prison, in a charitable capacity, of course. We *could* send Mr Giggs, but I do not wish to take him into our confidence unless we have to.'

Lucasta looked up quickly.

'Mr Giggs is here?'

The viscount nodded.

'Yes. Unfortunately, he arrived late this afternoon.'

The duchess shook her head at her godson.

'You are so uncharitable, Kennington. You need not worry

about Mr Giggs, Lucasta: he is such a heavy sleeper he will know nothing of your being here.'

Lucasta swallowed.

'I am quite ready to go back to Newgate, ma'am.'

'Good girl.'

'And I tell you we should not send Miss Symonds to such a place,' declared the viscount.

'Potts will accompany her, she will be perfectly safe.' The duchess smiled at Lucasta. 'I shall give you a purse, my dear, for you will have to pay the gaolers, and you had best take a hackney carriage: it would not do for you to arrive in my coach. Now, do you think you can do it?'

'Yes, indeed, ma'am. I am so pleased to be able to help.'

'Well, I am not!' declared the viscount. 'And we have not yet heard why the devil you thought it necessary to prowl around Cheapside in those clothes!'

'I knew you wouldn't like it,' muttered Jacob with grim satisfaction.

'Like it? Of course I don't like it! Bad enough, Jacob, that you should be keeping an eye on Miesel, but that you should encourage Miss Symonds—'

'Now that I never did!' exclaimed Potts, putting up his hands. 'I couldn't rein her in, my lord: she threatened to go it alone if I refused to help her!'

'Yes, you must not blame Jacob,' put in Lucasta. 'I was determined to search Miesel's rooms and—'

'You actually broke into his rooms?' The viscount clapped a hand to his head. 'Of all the foolish things to do—'

'No I did *not* break in. I did not need to because there is no lock on his door.'

'But did you not think what might happen if you had been caught?'

'No, I was too busy thinking of you!' she retorted, angry

colour springing to her cheeks.

'Very laudable I am sure, but what if Miesel had come back?'

'Well, he didn't and I found the emeralds!' At last she had silenced him. 'I f-found the necklace hidden under the floorboards.'

'May I ask why you did not tell Mr Loughton this?'

His cold tone depressed her. She suddenly felt very tired. Jacob came to her aid.

'We thought he might suspect us of putting it there,' he said. 'Now we know Miesel has it, Miss Symonds thinks we should set a trap for him.'

'An excellent idea,' agreed the duchess, 'but it is far too late to do any such thing now. Potts, we shall have a room prepared for you. And Lucasta, would you like to stay here? I have no doubt we can find some excuse to offer your mother in the morning.'

'Thank you, ma'am, but I think I must go back before I am missed.'

'Very well, I shall order my carriage for you.'

Lucasta felt too exhausted to argue. She sat back in her chair, trying to ignore the viscount's frowns. It seemed so unfair that he should be angry with her when she had tried so hard to help him. She hoped it would not take too long to summon the carriage from the mews; she was afraid she would fall asleep in the chair.

'If you will permit me, Your Grace,' said Jacob, 'I will escort Miss Symonds back to Sophia Street.'

'Now why should you want to do that?' demanded Adam.

'Because if she wants to get back in the way she came out, she will need help to get over the wall, is that not so, miss?'

'Yes, thank you, Jacob.'

'Get yourself to bed, Jacob, I will take Miss Symonds home.'

Lucasta glared at the viscount.

'You need not trouble yourself,' she said icily. 'One of the footmen can come with me.'

'Now you are being childish as well as foolish!'

'Not at all! And pray tell me how you intend to come with me when you are being watched? Do you want General Bradfield to know you helped me climb over a wall?'

'Peace, children! Lucasta, you will leave as you should do by the front door. Adam will be waiting for you on the corner of the street – I will not explain any further, you must trust me when I tell you that there is more than one exit that may be used after dark. Hurry now. I think perhaps you should change if you are going out, Adam.' A laugh trembled in the duchess's voice. 'And perhaps you would fetch a wrapper for Lucasta. I fear it will be growing cold.'

Lucasta clambered into the elegant carriage and slumped into the heavily padded seat. When they stopped a few moments later to pick up Lord Kennington she pulled the duchess's warm cloak tightly around her, unwilling to have any contact with the viscount. The coach pulled away again and in the darkness she heard him chuckle.

'Cry friends with me, Luke. This offended air does not become you.'

'Why should I be offended?' she forced herself to say lightly.

'Because I chastised you for your recklessness, instead of falling at your feet in gratitude.'

She sniffed. With a sigh he reached out and pulled her to him, cradling her stiff, unyielding body against his while he rested his cheek against her hair.

'I *am* grateful, you know, but the thought of you putting yourself in danger like that makes my blood run cold. I cannot bear to think of anything happening to you.'

'Is that true?'

She pulled away a little and stared up at him. The light was so poor inside the carriage that his face was little more than a pale blur and a gleam of white teeth as he laughed.

'Of course.' He kissed the tip of her nose and pulled her close to him again. 'I would hate anything to happen to my little friend.'

She subsided against him, sighing. He had called her his friend. She squeezed her eyelids together tightly to hold back the tears.

Lord Kennington insisted she keep the cloak wrapped around her as they walked along the alley to the back of the house. A half moon was riding high overhead, bathing everything in a soft grey light.

'Are you sure you will be able to get in?'

'Yes. I locked the door when I came out and put the key under a stone.'

'Come along then.'

'Goodnight, my lord.'

She handed him the cloak and stood, looking up at him. He bent his head and brushed her lips with his own. Lucasta dug her nails into her palms to restrain herself from throwing her arms about his neck. It was only another friendly kiss, after all.

'Goodnight, Lucasta.'

He cupped his hands to form a step for her and she scrambled over the wall, dropping lightly to the ground on the other side. She found the key where she had left it and silently let herself into the house.

When she reached her room she went straight to the window to extinguish the light. Peering out, her eyes searched the alley, but it was deserted.

CHAPTER TWENTY-ONE

When the hackney cab turned into Sophia Street the following morning Lucasta was waiting, dressed in her most sober
gown and wearing a serviceable woollen cloak over all. She
ran down the steps as the carriage came to a halt, but pulled
up sharply and was obliged to smother a gasp as the door
opened and Lord Kennington jumped out.

'What are you doing here? I thought Jacob was going with
me.'

'I thought it would be better if I came with you.' He
handed her into the carriage and jumped in after her.

'But I thought you were being watched.'

'*Lord Kennington* is being followed everywhere, but when
Giggs arrived yesterday he did so in such state that the
watchers could not fail to notice him. So I – er – borrowed a
hat and one of his coats to go out. I no longer look like a
viscount, do I?'

She stared at his plain black frock coat and the wide-
brimmed hat crammed onto his head.

'You look like a parson,' she told him, trying not to laugh.

'Thank you.' He grinned. 'I was afraid Lady Symonds
would come out to see you off and I should have to explain
why I was dressed like a cleric today.'

'I told her I was going out on charitable work for the duchess.' She sighed. 'Poor Mama is by now resigned to my alliance with your family and she does not remonstrate with me, merely rolls her eyes and utters dire warnings of my dragging the whole family into disgrace.'

'Oh I hope it will not come to that,' he replied, startled.

'Of course it will not.' She chuckled. 'I have told her she may put it about that I am out of my wits. I expect when this is over she will have me carried off to Bedlam.'

'You need not fear I shall allow that: if the worst happens I shall find you a small cottage on one of my estates where you may live in comfortable retirement!'

'Like Viola.'

'What was that?'

'I shall make me a willow cabin at your gate . . . pay me no heed, Adam. I am merely being fanciful.'

They had arrived at Newgate and the carriage pulled up in the shadows of one of the stark, high prison walls. As Adam handed Lucasta out of the carriage she shivered. He squeezed her fingers.

'Frightened?'

She managed a tight smile.

'Not nearly so much as I was the first time. I have you with me.'

'And I will take care of you. Come along now.'

The viscount's sober garb might not command the same obsequious attention as his usual velvet and gold lace, but the judicious application of coin soon opened the doors to them and they were led away into the depths of the prison.

It was soon borne upon Lucasta that there was a great difference between visiting a rich gentleman in a private cell and calling out of charity upon the poorest inmates. Although much of the building was relatively new, the heavy wooden doors with their iron bands and studs reminded her of some medieval fortress. They followed the turnkey along a maze of narrow, twisting stone passages, heavy doors unlocked and secured again behind them until they reached the crowded cells. There was no heating and on the cold spring day the chill in the passages struck into Lucasta's bones, even through her thick layers of clothing. The stench of filth and rotting decay made her gag and she stumbled, putting out her hand to steady herself. Adam caught her fingers and held them in a firm, sustaining clasp.

'Do you want to go back?' he asked her.

'No,' her voice was muffled by the handkerchief she held to her face. 'No, I shall not collapse, I assure you.'

They carried on. The food and clothes the duchess had provided were soon given out and Lucasta's heart ached to see the prisoners fighting each other for a share of the bounty, the scrawny dogs that lived inside the prison snapping at their heels.

'I understand you have recently taken in another inmate,' remarked the viscount.

The gaoler rubbed his nose with one grubby finger.

'Well now, we are always takin' in new prisoners,' he said with a toothy grin.

'But this is a young man from Worcestershire, I believe. Accused of murder.'

'You mean that despicable murder on Hansford Common? Oh, aye, they brought him in. He's this way.'

The turnkey took them past a bare, barred courtyard until they reached another large cell. Dozens of prisoners were to be seen, shadowy figures in a twilight world, for the light from the high window did little to brighten the heavy stone walls or the inmates themselves, whose ragged clothes had lost their colour and were now merely various shades of grey. They were separated from the prisoners by two sets of iron gratings, set apart so that nothing could be handed across the divide. Some prisoners paced around like caged animals but many were heavily manacled and secured with chains stapled into the floor.

'Dear heaven,' murmured Lucasta, her heart going out to the poor wretches. 'Are such chains really necessary?'

'Maybe, maybe not.' Their guide laughed and spat on the floor. 'Certainly not if they can afford to pay. Everything here has its price. You were asking about the prisoner from Worcestershire. That's 'im.'

Lucasta followed his pointing finger. A slightly built young man was sitting against the wall, knees updrawn and his head resting on his arms. As if aware of their presence the figure raised a tousled head and stared at them with huge, dread-filled eyes. He was only a boy. Lucasta shuddered, horror and pity bringing her close to tears.

'May we talk with him, privately?'

The turnkey looked at them. Lucasta could read the speculation in his greedy eyes. The viscount pulled a purse out of his pocket and shook it, making the coins chink.

'Ten minutes in private. Methinks here is a soul worth saving.'

The turnkey held out his hand and Lord Kennington counted out the coins. Lucasta held her breath while the man considered. At last he nodded.

'Very well. This way.' He led them along to a door at the far end of the passage. It opened into a small room sparsely furnished with a table and two rickety chairs. 'Wait here. He will be brought to you.'

'Gaoler.' The viscount threw him another coin. 'Bring bread and wine, too.'

Lucasta inspected one of the chairs before sitting down.

'What a dreadful place,' she whispered. 'Pray God we do not have to come here again.'

'I should not have brought you.'

'No, I did not mean that! But . . . can they really think that poor boy is me?'

A smile flickered across the viscount's sober face.

'The landlord from the Pigeons would have described you as a scrawny, brown-haired lad: in that respect you and that poor wretch are alike.' He broke off as a slatternly woman entered with a tray bearing a hunk of bread, a jug and three horn mugs. The viscount poured out a little wine and tried it.

'Poor stuff, but better than nothing. Here, drink a little, Lucasta. It will put some heart into you.'

She shook her head, pressing her handkerchief closer to her mouth.

'The thought of taking any food or drink in this place makes me shudder.'

The clank of chains warned them that the prisoner was approaching. The boy stumbled in, heavy chains around his ankles and his wrists shackled together before him. Lucasta jumped up, trying to hide her own distress as she observed his white, frightened face.

The viscount gestured to the gaoler to leave them. He went out, clanging the door shut behind him.

'Do not be afraid,' said Lucasta, guiding the boy to a chair. 'We want to help you.'

The boy looked up at the viscount, a flicker of hope in his eyes.

'I didn't murder no one, sir, on my word!'

'Very well, then tell us everything.'

'First of all, pray tell us your name,' put in Lucasta.

'Jem,' muttered the boy. 'Jem Spetchley. I live with my

mother on the edge of the Common.' He looked up again suddenly. 'She's a widow, sir, and – and not wealthy. She has no money for – for lawyers, or to come to London.'

The viscount gave him a mug of the wine.

'Tell us why you were arrested.'

'I – I was trying to sell a snuff-box. I found it on the Common.'

'It belonged to Sir Talbot Bradfield?'

'Yes. But I didn't kill him!'

'Then tell us what happened.'

'I was on the Common that Friday. We have a couple of goats that we put out there for grazing sometimes. I had been checking on them when I heard a shot.'

'Just the one?'

'Aye, sir. I thought it might be footpads so I hid in the bushes, I was afraid of what they would do to me if I was seen. Anyway, it was very quiet, so I crept forwards and soon I comes across a fancy yellow carriage and the horses, just standing.' He took a gulp of wine. 'There – there was a man, lying on the ground with a – a pistol in his hand.'

'Did you touch him?'

The boy shook his head.

'No. He – he didn't move. He was dead. There was b-blood on his back, a big stain of it on his green coat. His – his eyes was open, staring.' He shuddered.' I just left him and ran home.'

'And what about the snuffbox?' asked Lucasta.

'That was lying on the ground some feet away. Pretty little box: I thought it would do no harm to take it – thought I could sell it for a few shillings, perhaps, but I didn't kill no one, ma'am, 'fore God I didn't.'

'Perhaps you are not telling us all the truth,' put in the viscount, watching him. 'Sir Talbot's dressing case was broken open and a number of valuable items taken.'

The boy looked up at him.

'I didn't see no case, sir. I didn't go near the carriage. I found the snuff box in the grass, like it had been dropped or thrown away.'

'So you went home.'

'Yes, sir.'

'And you did not think to call the constable?'

Jem's face crumpled.

'No. I was certain sure the man was dead, so there was no help for him, and – and I thought if I said anything... well, it was all over the village the next day, that a man had been shot by footpads on the Common.'

'And you tried to sell the snuffbox?'

'Yes, ma'am. I walked to Bromsgrove. I didn't think anyone there would know. . . .'

Lucasta looked up at the viscount, who nodded at her.

'General Bradfield was very thorough in advertising his reward.'

They heard the key scrape in the lock.

'That's it, you've had your time.' The gaoler came in, swinging his keys. 'I must take the prisoner back to 'is cell now.'

Jem gazed up piteously at the viscount.

'Can you not help me? Please, sir. . . .'

Lord Kennington nodded.

'We will do what we can for you. Do not lose hope, Master Spetchley.'

They watched him being escorted away.

'Adam, I—'

The viscount put up his hand and shook his head at her. She was obliged to keep to herself the thoughts and conjecture running riot in her head until they were safely in the carriage again and on their way back to Filwood House.

'Well, now,' mused the viscount. 'What do you make of it all? There are several points in Jem's story that do not tie up with the account the valet has given.'

'Adam, could the boy have been lying? I cannot believe it; he was far too frightened for that.'

'I agree. And Bradfield had his snuffbox in his pocket when we saw him at Bromsgrove.'

'Yes, but it could not have fallen *out* of his pocket when he was shot, certainly not to end up some feet away from the body.'

'My thoughts exactly.' The viscount nodded. 'I think it more likely that Sir Talbot had the snuffbox in his hand when he was killed. But a man doesn't stop to take snuff when he is under attack.'

'Jem said he heard only the one shot. But that is not possible; the weapon in Sir Talbot's hand had been recently fired, you told me so yourself.'

'Ah, but not necessarily by Bradfield.'

Lucasta stared at him, her eyes widening in horror as an alarming idea formed in her head.

'I think,' she began, 'I think Sir Talbot might have stepped down from the carriage and someone . . . someone shot him with the pistol, then put it in his hand.'

'That is my conclusion, too.'

'M-Miesel?'

'Everything points that way.'

'Oh good heavens! It was enough to think he would steal his master's goods, but this—' She reached out and gripped his arm. 'Adam, I know her grace is confident that you will be found not guilty, that with your riches and connections they will not convict you, but now that is not enough.'

'That was never enough,' he retorted. 'I am determined to clear my name.'

'Of course, but we must ensure that poor boy is set free, and I want to see Miesel brought to justice.'

'Then we had better think of a plan.'

CHAPTER TWENTY-TWO

At Filwood House they were shown up to the duchess's sitting-room and quickly informed her of their meeting with Jem Spretchley.

'The poor boy,' exclaimed Lucasta, when their report was finished. 'I cannot bear to think of him incarcerated there in my place.'

'He *did* steal the snuffbox,' the duchess reminded her.

'Yes, but to be accused of murder, and taken so far from his home.'

'Do not distress yourself, Lucasta.' Lord Kennington consoled her. 'An anonymous benefactor shall provide him with a few comforts such as a room to himself, and decent food. And I shall send someone to Worcestershire to take a report of Jem to his mother and to ensure she is not left wanting. Now if you will excuse me, ma'am, I will leave you to think it all over while I go and change: I cannot say I like these dismal clothes.'

Lucasta watched him stride out of the room.

'Does Mr Giggs know why he needed his coat and hat, ma'am?'

'No, he knows only that Adam wished to go out without being followed. And there is no need to worry that Mr Giggs will disturb us here, Lucasta: this is my private boudoir. No one comes in here without an invitation. But your visit to Newgate has upset you, I think.'

'It is a wretched place, ma'am. I believe this new building is a vast improvement on the old one, but conditions are still squalid: the poor souls are treated more like animals than people. Something needs to be done.'

'There are groups working for the improvement of such institutions,' replied the duchess.

'When all this is over I shall seek them out. There must be some way I can help, by writing letters, perhaps.'

'You could help them a great deal more if you married a wealthy man: rich and influential patrons are exceedingly useful in cases like these.'

Lucasta sighed.

'Since there is very little prospect of my marrying anyone, I must content myself with letter-writing.'

The duchess reached out one hand. She tilted Lucasta's chin up to look into her face.

'Are you so sure you are going to become an old maid?' she asked, smiling.

Lucasta looked away and murmured, a little wistfully, 'I have vowed, ma'am, that I shall not marry without love.'

She looked round as the viscount came back into the room, and in that unguarded moment her expression confirmed all the duchess's suspicions.

The Filwood carriage took Lucasta back to Sophia Street that afternoon, where she found her mother and sister preparing for their visit to the theatre. Lucasta was relieved that her family showed very little interest in how she had spent her morning, Camilla merely bemoaning it as a morning wasted and Lady Symonds having little time to spare for her since she was so preoccupied with guiding her younger daughter through the perils of her first Season.

Camilla was very much enjoying her come-out and her radiant beauty was attracting so many gentlemen that it was an easy matter for her to forget Lord Kennington's early claims to her affection. Her mother, however, had no wish to alienate the viscount just yet. Mentally running through the list of possible suitors, Lord Kennington was not the richest, but his was the only title above the rank of baronet and Lady Symonds would not have been human if she had not pictured her lovely daughter as a viscountess. But the viscount had the shocking spectre of a murder trial hanging over him, and until that was removed she would not allow Camilla to stand up for more than one dance with him, nor would she permit them to converse together for more than a few minutes. Such vigilance was very wearing, but she was relieved that the viscount appeared to accept the situation with a good grace and when he came to their box at the theatre that night to pay his respects, he did no more than bow to Camilla before turning to engage Lucasta in conversation. She greeted him with a smile as he bowed over her hand.

'How delightful to see you, my lord. Are you enjoying the play?'

'Very much.' He lowered his voice. 'Can I assume there are no repercussions from your recent . . . adventures?'

Her eyes danced.

'My mother will tell you that I was laid low with a headache all day yesterday and throughout the night, sir. This morning's charitable works evinced very little interest, I assure you.' She lowered her voice. 'Have there been any developments since we last met, my lord?'

'The duchess has been successful in securing Jacob's freedom although, like myself, he remains under investigation.'

'How irksome.' She unfurled her fan and studied the pattern. 'Did you know that Mr Potts has developed a liking for cheese?'

'Has he, by Gad? Now I think of it, he has spoken of a certain cheesemonger's in Milk Street.'

'I hope he will not be prevented from going there.'

'He might be, of course, if it was known that he was out, but you know there are ways of leaving Filwood House without attracting the attention of those employed to watch the doors.'

The ringing of the bell warned them all that the next play was about to start. The visitors took their leave and the viscount bowed once again over her hand.

'By the bye, Miss Symonds, pray do not be alarmed if you do not hear from me for a few days. Oh, and I almost forgot to mention it. There will be a notice in tomorrow's *Evening Post*. You might find it of interest.'

The viscount's parting comment left Lucasta in a state of seething indignation. It was surely deliberate that he had left this information until the last moment to avoid her questions. Lady Symonds did not consider it necessary to have a subscription to any newspaper while in Town and Lucasta was obliged to send a footman to purchase a copy for her the following day. She waited impatiently for his return, whereupon she carried the newssheet off to her room. It did not take her long to find the notice. Tucked between Mr Smyth's Restorative Medicine for Weakness & Debility at eleven shillings a bottle and an advertisement for a Cyprian Preventive against the horrible effects of a certain disease was a small paragraph:

Following the barbarous act of violence recently carried

out on Hansford Common, Worcs, on the 17th day of March this year, it is now understood that a lone rider was seen crossing that section of common at the time of the atrocity. Description: tall, approximately thirty years of age, very dark and dressed for travel. Possibly a foreigner. Any persons with knowledge of this gentleman should present their information to Sam'l Loughton at Bow Street Magistrates' Court, bearing in mind the reward offered for the conviction of the offender(s).

Lucasta stared at the notice. She began to nibble at her fingertip. A witness. Was it possible? And why had Adam not mentioned it when she asked him if there was any news? She was still deliberating when there was a knock on her door and her maid brought in a note from the Duchess of Filwood.

'Her footman is waiting downstairs for an answer, miss.'

Lucasta did not hesitate.

'Tell him yes, I would be delighted to drive out with the duchess tomorrow morning. I will be waiting for her at eleven o'clock.'

CHAPTER TWENTY-THREE

The familiar warmth of the tavern welcomed Dan Miesel as he entered the Raven, enveloping him with a smoky cloud in which the smell of sweat, tobacco, meat and onions mingled. He nodded at the landlord and made his way to his usual seat at the long table.

'There's a gennleman bin askin' after you.'

Miesel stopped and looked back at the landlord, suddenly alert.

'Oh? What sort of gentleman?'

The man shrugged, wiping his hands on his greasy apron.

'The foreign sort, I'd say.' He nodded. 'Over there, sittin' by the fire. Came in an hour since and said he'd wait for you.'

Miesel looked across the room. The poor light made it difficult to see across the smoky room but he could make out a greatcoated figure hunched over a small table near the fire. The lighted lamp on the mantelpiece threw the shadow from the wide brim of his hat across his face. On the table before him stood a wine bottle and a half-empty glass. Miesel hesitated.

'A foreigner, you say?'

His host sniffed.

'Aye, one o' they damned Frenchies, I don't doubt.'

Miesel looked again and, intrigued, made his way across the room until he was standing before the huddled figure.

'I am told you have been asking after me.'

The man raised his head. His hat still shadowed the upper portion of his face but Miesel could now see that his lean cheeks were dark with a few days' growth of beard.

'You are Miesel?'

The low voice was heavily accented.

'I am *Mister* Miesel. What do you want with me?'

The man reached into his pocket and pulled out a folded newssheet. He held it out. Miesel took the paper and moved closer to the lamp to read it. After several moments he bent a frowning look upon the stranger.

'Well? That is nothing to do with me.'

'*Vraiment, m'sieur*, I think it has everything to do with you.'

Miesel glanced back at the newspaper.

'Tall, dark, thirtyish—' His eyes narrowed. '*You* are the man seen on Hansford Common?'

'Per'aps.'

'Well, man?' He pulled up a chair and leaned closer. 'What did you see?'

The stranger did not move and after a few moments Miesel said, 'Perhaps we should discuss this over a jug of porter.'

The thin lip curled.

'As you wish, *m'sieur*.'

Miesel beckoned the serving maid over and barked out his instructions. Almost immediately a large jug and two horn cups were set down before him. He looked around, making sure there was no one close enough to hear them. Satisfied, he picked up the jug.

'Will you take a cup of ale with me, sir?'

158

'Thank you, no. I prefer the wine.'

'As you please. But if we are to continue I want to know your name, and your country – where do you hail from, France?'

'Aye, from the south, where there are warm winds and dry days.'

'And your name, sir?'

'Is it necessary?'

Miesel's thin, pointed face took on a stubborn look.

'Aye, I think so.'

The man shrugged.

'I am Alphonse Fôret. I am in your country to discuss the art of pot-making. Having concluded my business I visited friends in Worcestershire before setting out again for London. It was then that I met with an – ah – adventure most exciting.'

Miesel poured himself a generous cupful of the strong dark ale and drank it down. Refreshed, he sat back and regarded the shadowy figure.

'I wish you'd take off that damn'd hat.'

A smile was the only response.

'So, then, are you going to describe this adventure?'

'It was a Friday, was it not? A cold day, but not raining, I think, which is a pleasant change in this country. I was crossing the – ah, how do you say it? – crossing the heather in the afternoon.'

'You refer to Hansford Common?'

'Ah, yes, the common, that is it. The country on the north side is very flat, is it not? But there are bushes and low trees, plenty of cover to hide footpads – or a *cavalier*.'

Miesel sat very still.

'Go on.'

'I had been riding for some time and it was necessary for

me to – ah – make relief. Not knowing the road, I would not risk being caught with my breeches open so I rode a way from the main path into the seclusion of the trees. I was soon thankful for my precautions, for a yellow carriage came along.'

He paused and it was all Miesel could do to sit passively while the stranger refilled his wineglass.

'Alas for my composure, the carriage, she stopped. *Eh bien*, M'sieur Miesel, I have the choice: do I mount my horse and ride out from the bushes, or do I remain hidden and hope the carriage drives on again very soon. I decided to wait. Now, *m'sieur*, it becomes interesting. I hear a shot. When I look out again the driver of the carriage, *voilà*, he is lying dead on the road.'

Miesel swallowed and licked his dry lips.

'And did you see the footpads?'

'Alas, no.'

'Well, that is no matter. You must know that they have arrested the murderer.'

The shadowed face was lightened by a sudden grin.

'An English lord? I believe your justice is no better than ours, *m'sieur*: he will not be convicted, even if he is guilty. But I think they would find my evidence most interesting. You see, after hearing the shot, I saw the incident most curious.' The man leaned forward. Miesel could not see his eyes, but he could feel them boring into him. 'There was a manservant in the carriage and, as I looked out, I saw this servant placing a pistol in the dead man's hand.'

'Impossible.'

'Oh, but I assure you, *m'sieur*, it is what I saw, and I think this Samuel Loughton would be very interested to hear this, *non?*'

'So why have you come here, why not go to Bow Street?'

The man sat back, irritatingly at his ease.

'Well, now, you see, I am a traveller in your country: I am on my way back to France. I have no wish to become involved in your petty crimes. After all, our two countries are forever at war, *non*? What is it to me if one more Englishman is dead?'

A sly grin split Miesel's lean countenance.

'Aye, *m'sieur*. You have the right of it. Why should you bother yourself with our concerns? It can only lead to trouble, you being a Frenchie and all.'

'*Oui.*' The man pointed to the newspaper. 'Only now I cannot ignore it, for it appears that I was seen.'

'But you have said yourself, *m'sieur*, that you are on your way home. There is no need for you to become involved in this little matter.'

'Ah, I wish that I could believe you, M'sieur Miesel, but – if there is a witness to my being there, I must clear my name. If I return to France then, who knows? It may be thought that I was the killer.'

'Ah,' said Miesel, smiling, 'but you would be safe over the water by then, would you not?'

'And yet I have my good name to think of.' Monsieur Fôret sat back, one hand resting on the table and his long fingers drumming on the wooden surface. 'I am a businessman, *m'sieur.*'

'Now I understand you. What is your price?'

'There are reports that a fine necklace went missing.'

'There are many reports, *m'sieur*. One should not believe all one hears.'

'Of a certainty, *m'sieur*, one should rather believe the evidence of one's own eyes.'

There was a long silence. The Frenchman gave a soft laugh and leaned forward.

'Come now, we both know it would be impossible to sell the necklace in this country for many months, and the longer you keep it the greater the danger. Give it to me: I will make my escape and leave a trail that cannot be missed. It will be believed that I am the murderer and you will be free of all suspicion.' He poured the rest of the wine into his glass. 'You will then be free to sell off the rest of your master's trinkets.'

Miesel stared at him.

'By God, how much do you know?'

Monsieur Fôret lifted his head and for a moment the lamplight glinted in his cold eyes.

'Enough to hang you, *Mister* Miesel. *Eh bien*, do we have the bargain?'

CHAPTER TWENTY-FOUR

Never had the hours passed so slowly for Lucasta. A nervous excitement disturbed her sleep and she was relieved when morning came and she could leave her bed. When she told her mama that she was driving out with the duchess the news was met with no more than a fatalistic shrug, while Camilla was more interested in deciding which of the posies that had been delivered from her admirers she should wear to the ball that evening. Lucasta looked at the colourful little bunches spread out on the table.

'Is there one from Lord Kennington?' she asked.

'No, but he told me last night that he will not be attending.'

'No doubt you are relieved,' muttered Lucasta drily. 'You are always so cold to him.'

Camilla tossed her head, making her golden curls dance.

'Adam understands. He has told me he will not pay his addresses until his name has been cleared.' Her hand hovered over the flowers. 'They are all so pretty and yet I think I shall wear . . . these.' She picked up a delicate bundle of blue and white flowers. 'They will match my dress beautifully. How clever of Sir Hilary.'

'Very clever,' laughed her mama, 'when you were anxious

to describe your gown to him in so much detail the other evening!'

As Lady Symonds sailed out of the room Lucasta looked at her sister.

'Camilla, do pray be serious for a moment and tell me truly what you feel for Adam. If – if your feelings towards him have changed, would it not be kinder to tell him now, than to let him go on hoping?'

'Oh, Sister, my feelings have not changed at all, and once he is free of all this scandal I shall be delighted to become engaged to him.' She began to dance about the room. 'Just think, Lucasta. I shall be a viscountess!'

'Yes, but do you love him?'

'Lord, Sister, of course I do!' She stopped dancing. 'Because I go out to parties every night does not mean I do not care what happens to Adam. I feel quite sad every time I think of him, but I know he does not want me to sit at home pining for him. Now I must go and stand these flowers in a bowl of water, or they will be dreadfully wilted by tonight.'

'Well, Your Grace, what can you tell me of this new witness?'

Lucasta had struggled to maintain a calm silence while the footman handed her into the carriage and carefully spread the rug across her knees, but as soon as they were trotting out of Sophia Street she could contain herself no longer.

'I know nothing of him, my dear, save what is written in the notice that was sent to the newspapers.'

Lucasta's eyes narrowed: she knew enough of the duchess to be wary of that mischievous smile.

'The report said he was seen on the common at the time of the murder. How is that known?' she lowered her voice to a whisper. '*Does he even exist?*'

The duchess's smile grew.

'How suspicious you are, my child. He must surely exist, since he was seen on Hansford Common. I think you should put up your parasol: the sun is particularly hot today.'

Lucasta did as she was bid, but immediately returned to the subject, saying quietly, 'Is this perhaps a result of Mr Loughton's investigations?'

The duchess gave a peal of merry laughter.

'Heavens, no. Mr Loughton was not at all pleased that I had used his name in the notice, but he has promised that he will not deny this report, should anyone question him about it. After all, as he so wisely said to me, "What is there to deny? It merely asks anyone with information to bring it to me at Bow Street and that is just what they should do, whether it is about a – er – foreign gentleman or anyone else". Really, I was quite impressed with him.'

'But if there is such a person, he may well have seen who attacked Sir Talbot: he would know that it was not Adam.'

'He would most assuredly know that Adam is innocent.'

Lucasta looked at the duchess, frowning a little. 'Is that why Lord Kennington is gone out of Town?'

The duchess opened her eyes at her.

'*Has* my godson left Town?'

Lucasta waved an impatient hand.

'There is no need to deny it, ma'am: he told me as much at the play the other night. Where has he gone, Your Grace? Is he hunting down this new witness? Is he gone to Hansford, perhaps?'

'Hush, Lucasta. Let us not speculate any further upon this matter. Be assured that when there is some news, some real news, I shall tell you of it.'

With this promise Lucasta had to be content, although she

found it hard to settle to anything for the rest of the day, and was glad when the time came to prepare for the evening's entertainment.

'Really Lucasta, you seem very eager to go out,' remarked Lady Symonds, as they went upstairs together. 'All this talk of your not wishing to go abroad, I knew it was all nonsense. You are not so very different from your sister: I knew you would come to enjoy yourself if you only put in a little effort.'

Lucasta shook her head, laughing, but she did not disagree. She wanted to attend all the balls and evening parties with her sister, eager to hear what was being said about Adam, however painful it might be. By forcing herself to go into society, she found that she had gradually overcome most of the awkwardness she felt on such occasions. In addition to this, most of the new acquaintances she met were so dazzled by Camilla that she no longer had the impression of being weighed up and assessed. If only Adam had been free of suspicion she thought she might even have enjoyed herself. As Lucasta accompanied her mother and sister into yet another ballroom, the knowledge that Adam would not be present doused her in a wave of disappointment. Camilla laughed, danced and flirted in her usual manner. If anything, she seemed even more vivacious, thought Lucasta: as if she was relieved that the viscount's disturbing presence had been removed.

Lucasta found the evening even more trying than usual, for all the talk was of the new witness. It seemed that the notice had been placed in every newspaper. Even Camilla was obliged to listen to comment upon it, for Lucasta heard Sir Hilary Collingham discussing the latest development as he escorted Camilla back to her party after a particularly energetic bourrée.

'A reliable witness is the very thing,' he remarked, his

round, boyish face glowing with the exercise of the dance. 'Kennington will be very glad to have that. I hope they track the fellow down as soon as maybe, then we can bring this sorry business to a close.'

'You believe the viscount to be innocent, Sir Hilary?' asked Lucasta, warming to the young man.

'Indeed I do, Miss Symonds. I've known the viscount for years, never known him do an ungentlemanly thing.'

'But the evidence,' sighed Camilla.

'Damn the evidence – begging your pardon, ladies,' exclaimed Sir Hilary. 'Even if I saw Kennington do such a thing with my own eyes I should still think there must be some reason for it. A man don't change, Miss Symonds, and that's a fact.'

Sir Hilary's words cheered Lucasta and it was in a sunnier mood that she joined her mother and sister at the breakfast table the following morning. However, she could persuade neither of them to stir out of the house before noon to accompany her to the circulating library, so she left them yawning over their coffee cups and set off with only her maid for company. She was crossing Hanover Square when she saw Jacob Potts watching her from the corner of one of the streets. She hailed him cheerfully and stopped to wait for him to come up to her.

'Good day to you, Mr Potts. How is your leg today?'

'It's healing nicely, miss, I thank you. I hardly limp at all now, you will notice.'

'I do, sir, and wonder that you do not look more happy about it.' She hesitated. 'I am on my way to Bond Street: will you not give me your company? Hannah will drop behind.' She smiled at the maid who gave her a speculative look.

'I ain't sure the mistress would like that, miss.'

Lucasta's lips twitched, knowing Hannah was calculating how much her silence was worth.

'Well, we will discuss it with Lady Symonds when we get back,' she said pleasantly, the steely look in her eye making it quite clear that there was no possibility of bribes on this occasion. She walked on, slowing her pace a little to accommodate Jacob's dragging step.

'So, Mr Potts, I thought you would have gone out of Town with Lord Kennington.'

'Aye, miss, that's what I would've thought, too,' grumbled the groom. 'But I'm to stay, to make it look as if his lordship is skulking in Filwood House.'

'But surely the general's men who are watching the house will grow suspicious if they do not see the viscount himself.'

'Ah, but they *do* see him.' Potts allowed himself a little smile. He glanced about to make sure there was no one within earshot. 'The watchers do see him, miss. Every so often the duchess has one of her trusted lackeys put on Lord Kennington's coat and parade in front of the window.'

'Good heavens!'

'Aye, fooled 'em proper, she has, for his lordship slipped out and is now heaven knows where and mayhap getting himself into all sorts of bother without me.' His mouth worked as if he was gathering himself up to spit, then he thought better of his company and merely sighed.

Lucasta's lips twitched as his despondency and she said in a bracing tone, 'The duchess and Lord Kennington know what they are about and I am sure they will tell us in good time. But tell me, have you visited Milk Street recently? Is the cheesemonger flourishing?'

It was a lucky shot: Jacob straightened himself.

'Aye, it happens that I have been buying a fair bit o' cheese recently. As a matter o' fact, I was there yesterday.'

'And how is Mistress Jessop?' Lucasta observed his suspicious look and added hastily, 'I greatly admire her, a woman alone, running a business.'

'She has a fine head on her shoulders,' agreed Jacob.

And a fine pair of shoulders, Lucasta added silently, remembering the ease with which the widow had moved the great cheeses. She dragged her thoughts back to more serious matters.

'But are you not afraid that you will be discovered? Would it not look suspicious if you were seen so close to Miesel's lodgings?'

'Lord love you, those watching Filwood House don't know I'm gone, and the ones keepin' an eye on Miesel haven't got the sense to look at anyone else! I changes me coat, puts on a hat and winds a muffler around me neck and they wouldn't recognize me from Adam. In fact,' he scowled suddenly, 'I didn't see anyone watching Miesel at all yesterday, and I was there for most o' the day.'

'All that time buying cheese?' murmured Lucasta at her most innocent.

'One of the windows in the back room was broken and I fixed it, that's all.'

'Yes, of course you did,' she said, a laugh trembling in her voice. 'Any gentleman would do the same. Pray do not mind me, Mr Potts. Do carry on.'

His reproving look almost overset her gravity, but she averted her eyes, staring hard at the pavement until he continued.

'Well, anyway, as I was saying I was in Milk Street most o' the day, and saw no one hanging around outside at all. So when Miesel takes himself off to the Raven for his dinner I follows him. No one knows who I am, o' course, but having been in the tavern on a couple of occasions no one takes any notice o' me, now, so I takes a flagon of porter and sits meself down quietly in one corner, watching Miesel. Well, blow me if he doesn't eat up his dinner then announces that he's off. An appointment, he says. That made me sit up a bit, and I took meself out into the street before he had settled up, so it didn't look like I was following him. Then I hung around on the corner until he came out.'

'And where did he go?'

'Whitechapel, miss. Very shady place. It wouldn't be too strong to say it was in the rookeries.'

'And you followed him there? Oh Jacob, what if he had seen you?'

'No need to look so grim, miss; there wasn't no danger of that. It was drizzling and Miesel had his head down so he wasn't paying attention. But since I could see no one else keeping an eye on our friend I thought it might prove useful.'

'Where did he go?'

'I followed him to this low tavern. There he gets into conversation with a group of pretty ugly characters. I daren't get too close, but they looked very much as if they were up to no good, so I keeps me ears pinned and stays in the corner with a flash o' lightning (that'd be gin to you). Then Miesel gets up to go, and I hear him say, quiet-like, "Do not forget, Finsbury Fields tomorrow – eight o'clock".'

'Heavens! And did you tell Lord Kennington about this?'

'Didn't have a chance, miss. He's been gone for a couple of days.'

'The duchess, then.'

'Well, I was going to, then I thought p'raps I should tell this Mr Loughton, so when he came round to check up on us all I mentioned it to him, and gets ticked off for me pains! He objected to my giving his men the slip.'

'But *did* he listen to you: is he going to have Miesel followed?'

Jacob aimed a kick at a stone on the flagway.

'He tells me that his men knows their business, which was to tell me to mind my own, if you ask me.'

'But we know that Miesel is a villain.'

'Aye,' he retorted gloomily. 'And he's up to more mischief, you mark my words.'

Lucasta fixed him with a steady, determined gaze.

'Then we must find out what it is, Jacob!'

CHAPTER TWENTY-FIVE

Lady Symonds regarded Lucasta in her riding habit and gave a sigh of resignation.

'So you are out again.'

'Yes. The duchess sends her groom and a mount for me.' She crossed her fingers behind her back: she hoped her mother would not recognize Potts as the viscount's groom rather than a member of the duchess's staff.

'I suppose it would be futile to tell you to keep your distance.'

'Completely, Mama,' replied Lucasta cheerfully.

'Your new habit looks very fine,' remarked her sister. 'It shows your figure to great advantage, and the colour suits you: nut brown was an excellent choice. I hope you are not planning to flirt with Kennington.'

A slight flush tinged Lucasta's cheek.

'I have no expectation of seeing the viscount, Camilla. You know very well that he is out of Town at present.'

'Well, it would do you no good if you did,' replied Camilla waspishly. 'He is violently in love with me.'

'And if you wish to keep his love perhaps you should show him a little more attention when you next meet!'

'Girls, pray stop your bickering! Lucasta, I see a groom in

the street, and leading a very fine horse, too. It will be the duchess's man: you had best be off.'

Lucasta dropped a swift kiss upon her mother's powdered cheek.

'If her grace asks me to stay for dinner it would be impolite of me to refuse, Mama. Pray do not be alarmed if I am not back by dusk.'

Lady Symonds sank back in her chair and put her hand over her eyes.

'You will not be satisfied until you have dragged us all into disgrace, I know it.'

'No, no, Mama, how can you think that? Besides, when Lord Kennington is proved innocent you will be glad we did not sever the connection.'

'If he is proved innocent.'

'Sir Hilary was quite confident of the outcome,' remarked Camilla.

Lady Symonds snorted.

'Sir Hilary is a fool.'

Camilla's blue eyes flashed.

'Mama, how can you say so? He was very attentive towards us last night. Yes, and you were most gracious – it is not seemly for you to disparage him in this way.'

'Well, he is a very genial fool, and a rich one, too, I'll grant you that. But I think you will find he is in the minority, supporting Kennington. Most people prefer to keep their counsel.'

Lucasta picked up her gloves.

'Most people are hypocrites,' she said bitterly. 'When Kennington is acquitted they will all declare they never for a moment doubted his innocence.'

'That is the way of the world, Lucasta, and you would do well to conform.'

'Not if it means going against my conscience!'

With a swish of her skirts Lucasta whisked herself out of the room.

'And who's been setting you in a high dudgeon, if you will forgive me for asking,' muttered Jacob, as he threw her up into the saddle.

'It does not matter. Oh, I beg your pardon, Jacob, I should not be uncivil to you because I am out of temper. Let us talk of other things. This is a fine mare, does the duchess ride her?'

'Aye, miss, this is one of her grace's favourite hacks. She was bred at Filwood. The old duke established an excellent stud farm there.'

'And does the present duke continue the tradition?'

Jacob did not answer until he was firmly mounted upon his own horse.

'Aye, although he doesn't keep the racing stock any longer, being of a more cautious nature.'

'I'd wager that does not please her grace.' She observed his hesitation and laughed. 'I shall not press you to answer that, Jacob. I would not have you criticize either the duchess or her son. Tell me instead if you have spoken to Mr Loughton.'

'No, miss. I called at Bow Street, as we agreed, but he was not there and they would not tell me when he was expected. But I did leave a message for him.'

'Then we can do no more. Perhaps he is at Hansford with the viscount. If that is the case then we have no choice: we must go to Finsbury Fields ourselves to see what is afoot.'

She set her horse to a trot and was soon leaving the familiar, fashionable streets behind. They rode eastwards towards the city before Jacob turned north and led the way past the old Artillery ground and on through narrow, decaying streets with rickety housing and the occasional burst of new building work.

'Only a little way now, miss. Finsbury Fields are just past the almshouse here. Look, you can see the windmills.'

She stared at the majestic towers with their huge sails.

'What business could Miesel have here, I wonder?'

'There's an inn a little way on, miss: perhaps he's going there.'

'Well we cannot go in and ask. I do not wish to draw attention to ourselves.'

They rode on and soon the road turned to a rutted lane, the houses disappeared and they found themselves riding between straggling hedges with large open fields stretching away to each side. They were buffeted by the sharp wind and the only sound was the swish from the sails of the windmills.

'Heavens, what a bleak place!' Lucasta exclaimed, pulling up the collar of her riding jacket.

'And it will be even bleaker, soon, for the mills will shut down at dusk, and every law-abiding person will be going home to his bed.'

'Then perhaps we should make ourselves less conspicuous,' suggested Lucasta, looking around her. 'Look, the windmill over there is already stopped and everything closed up. If we go behind the tower we will not be visible from the road.'

'Just what are we expecting to see?' asked Potts, following her across the field.

'Well, I do not know, but if Miesel is up to no good, it cannot do any harm to know of it. This is perfect; the elevated position gives us an excellent view of the fields and the lane running through the middle. Now, we have about an hour until dusk, and when the light begins to fail, no one will see us here. Let us dismount: I prefer to spend the waiting time sitting on a tree stump than in the saddle.'

Kicking her foot from the stirrup Lucasta slipped nimbly to the ground but instead of sitting down she walked up and down, tapping her riding whip impatiently against her skirts. Potts tethered the horses and sat down on an empty barrel. He took out a small packet and began to unwrap it. She stopped her pacing and watched him.

'More cheese, Jacob?'

'Aye, tasty it is, too. From Lancashire, I'm told. It goes well with a glass o' Nants – that's brandy, miss, and I just happens to have a flask in my saddle-bag, should we feel the cold later.'

'You are becoming an expert on cheeses.' Her lips curved into a smile. 'Perhaps you have a yearning to go into the business?'

'Aye, well, that I might, one day.'

She laughed at him.

'I wish you joy then, Jacob.' She turned again to look out over the fields. 'It seems very busy now.'

A number of figures were moving along the lane.

'Mayhap they are returning from market,' suggested Jacob.

'Mayhap.' Lucasta peered into the twilight. 'Although they seem to be moving off the path . . . yes, they are going into the woods.' Suddenly, her heart was beating hard. 'Jacob, if you were going to lie in wait for someone, where would you choose to do it?'

He put the cheese back into his pocket and came to stand beside her.

'Down there, where the road runs between the trees.'

'Did you recognize any of them?'

'Not from this distance. They could be footpads . . . perhaps we should go back. . . .'

'No, indeed. We must wait to see what happens.' She shivered in the cold wind. 'Although I do wish I had worn a surcoat.'

'But this could get dangerous. Let us go back to the inn and fetch help.'

She shook her head.

'If we leave here now we would be seen. Besides, it is growing dark, and we might miss something.'

'I wish I had never agreed to this,' muttered Potts miserably.

'There is nothing to be afraid of, Jacob.'

He drew himself up, saying indignantly, 'I ain't afraid, miss, leastways not for meself, but her grace will never forgive me if you was to be in danger, and with only me to protect you.'

She gave him a mischievous look.

'I can protect myself.' She reached into the pocket beneath her voluminous skirts and pulled out a pistol.

'Lord a' mercy! Never tell me that thing is loaded.'

'But of course it is, and you know I can use it, you said so yourself, on Hansford Common.'

'Aye, and what a deuce of a pickle we have been in since then!' He shook his head at her. 'I'm only a servant and can't order you to leave here, miss, but I wish you would go. I wish to goodness my lord was here!'

Lucasta sighed.

'I wish that, too,' she murmured.

As the light faded the wind grew colder. One by one the huge windmills stopped working, their huge sails turned on edge to the wind and silence descended over the fields, broken only by the creak and rattle of timbers buffeted by the breeze. Jacob shivered.

'It is well nigh dark now, miss. Eight o'clock must be past by now and nothing has occurred. We should go back.'

Lucasta looked down towards the trees. Nothing was stirring.

'Perhaps you are right. Perhaps those men were merely on their way home.' She sighed. 'Very well, Jacob. Help me to mount, please.'

'Am I to take you back to Sophia Street, Miss Symonds?'

'Yes.' She settled herself in the saddle, rearranging her skirts while she waited for the groom to climb onto his own horse. 'Oh dear, it will be so late when we get back that I shall be obliged to tell Mama I dined at Filwood House. How hungry I shall be by then! Perhaps you would let me have the rest of that cheese, Jacob—'

'Hush, miss! Look.'

He pointed towards the lane. A solitary rider was approaching. Even in the low light she could see he was wrapped up well against the night air in a travelling cloak, his hat pulled down over his face.

'That cannot be Miesel,' said Potts. 'The man is much too tall.'

They watched the rider disappear into the shadowy darkness of the trees. Then there was a cry, the sudden neighing of a horse.

'It is an attack. Quickly, Jacob!'

'Should we ride for help, miss?'

'No, that would take too long.' She pulled the pistol from her skirts. 'We must go and help.'

Ignoring the groom's protests, she set her horse at a gallop towards the trees.

Lucasta could hear nothing above the thud of her horses' hoofs and the wind whistling around her, but as she reached

the lane there were sounds of a commotion. The road disappeared into the shadowy tunnel of the overhanging trees.
Peering ahead, she could just make out several figures
struggling together in the darkness. A riderless horse
hovered nervously at the side of the road. It was too dark to
see clearly, so Lucasta raised her pistol and fired into the air.

For a moment the struggling figures froze, but as Potts
came thundering up behind her they took to their heels and
fled. Only one remained. The traveller was lying face down
and motionless on the ground.

'Oh, pray heaven he is not dead!' whispered Lucasta,
jumping down.

'Be careful miss!'

Jacob's warning went unheeded as Lucasta fell to her
knees beside the still figure. She leaned over him.

'He breathes! Help me turn him, Jacob.'

With some difficulty they rolled the man onto his back,
Lucasta gently cradling his dark head on her skirts.

'He is coming around, Jacob. Will you fetch your brandy
flask, if you please? No, do not try to move, yet, sir. We need
to ascertain how badly you are hurt.'

She looked down into the bearded face and smiled reas-
suringly even though it was doubtful he could see her in the
darkness. She did not know how he would react: confused,
perhaps, or gasping with pain. She was not prepared for the
blazing anger when he spoke to her.

'You interfering baggage! What the *devil* do you think you
are doing?'

CHAPTER TWENTY-SIX

Lucasta was so shocked her hands fell away from him.

'Adam!'

He sat up, groaning slightly as he did so.

'And who else did think it would be? What the devil are you doing here if you didn't follow me?'

As Potts came back at that moment she was not obliged to answer. The groom's relief at finding his master was evident and he held out the flask, bidding my lord to drink as much as he wanted.

'I'm mightily pleased to see you, my lord. Very pleased indeed.'

'You won't be so pleased when I've finished with you,' growled the viscount. 'What the devil do you mean by bringing Miss Symonds into such danger?'

'Now you are being unfair, my lord,' cried Lucasta. 'And ungrateful too, when we have come to your rescue!'

'I did not need you to come to my rescue. Help is at hand, I needed only to hold out for a moment longer.'

'When I arrived you were unconscious on the ground!'

'Only because I was distracted by that damned pistol-shot—'

'Someone's approaching!'

Jacob's warning silenced them.

'All's well,' muttered the viscount, getting to his feet. 'It is Loughton.'

Lucasta jumped up.

'Mr Loughton? What is he doing here?'

'He was looking out for me. Well, did you catch them?'

'Aye, my lord.' Loughton trotted up to them. 'I thought we was going to be too late, for I missed the way and we ended up at Frog Lane, but we was just coming up to the wood when they ran straight into us. And only too willing to blab. From what they have already told me we can safely arrest Miesel and, if he still has the necklace, that will wrap it up nicely. I have left my men to bind em up tight and take 'em back to Bow Street while I came to see that you was not hurt.'

'Do you mean to tell me you planned this?' demanded Lucasta, staring.

'Aye,' replied the Runner. 'Well, apart from the fact that we was meant to be following closer to his lordship, to be ready for any attack, you see.'

'Well, you were not ready, and that was very remiss of you,' put in Lucasta crossly. 'Lord Kennington might have been killed if he had been obliged to wait for you to turn up.'

'One might ask just what you are doing here, Miss Symonds,' retorted Loughton, bristling. 'And you, Potts: you are still under suspicion, don't forget.'

'I think we should postpone this discussion,' put in the viscount. 'Miss Symonds is shivering. Here.' He shrugged off his greatcoat and draped it around her shoulders.

'Thank you.' She tried to read his expression in the darkness. 'Are you sure you are not hurt?'

'Nothing more than a few cuts and bruises.' His hands rested on her shoulders and Lucasta knew an impulse to

181

step forward and cling on to him, to reassure herself that he was truly alive. Then the moment was gone and he was saying briskly, 'There is an inn a little way back down the road. Potts, you can come there with me while Loughton escorts Miss Symonds back to Sophia Street.'

Angrily, she pulled away from him.

'I will not go home until you have told me what is going on.'

'Do not be so foolish, Lucasta. You cannot be seen in a common inn.'

'This is as much my adventure as yours now. Besides, you are in my debt: I have just saved your life.'

In the tense silence she heard Mr Loughton chuckle.

'She has you there, my lord. Perhaps we can hire a private parlour, and grease the landlord's palm to stand mum about it.'

'An excellent plan, Mr Loughton.' Lucasta walked over to her mare and took up the reins. 'Please throw me up, Jacob.'

But it was the viscount who marched forward and tossed her up into the saddle.

'You are dangerously headstrong, Lucasta. Quite heedless of your reputation.'

'My reputation is none of your concern,' she flashed.

'No, thank God.'

They rode in silence to the inn, where Mr Loughton went in first to procure a private room for them. Despite Lucasta's protests the viscount threw his coat over her head and hustled her past the tap room door, only releasing her from his vice-like grip once they were safely inside the private parlour. She threw off the greatcoat and glared at him.

'That was quite unnecessary, my lord. I am not known in this area.'

'And I want it to remain that way.'

182

Mr Loughton coughed.

'Perhaps, ma'am, you would like to sit down and I will pour you a glass of wine?'

'Yes, thank you.'

'I think we should all sit down,' muttered the viscount.

Mr Loughton guided Lucasta to one of the rickety chairs beside the table, requested the viscount to take the other, assuring him that the three-legged stools would be perfectly suitable for himself and Mr Potts.

'Now,' barked the viscount, when they were all seated. 'Jacob, you will explain yourself, if you please!'

Lucasta opened her mouth to object, but as she met the groom's eye he gave a tiny shake of his head, warning her to remain silent. She closed her lips again. Perhaps it was best for Jacob to speak to his master, since everything she said to the viscount seemed to inflame him.

While the groom explained how he had followed Miesel and overheard his conversation in the Whitechapel tavern, Lucasta leaned back in the chair, cradling her glass of wine between her hands. In the safety of the well-lighted room and with a fire crackling merrily in the hearth, her jangled nerves grew steadier. She found herself studying Lord Kennington. The dark bag-wig and rough beard that covered half his face gave him the look of a stranger. Even his grey eyes had lost their usual smile and appeared darker. She looked closer. The areas of his face not hidden by hair were cut and bruised from his recent beating. She had seen at least four attackers. Had he really been fighting them off successfully before she intervened? The thought of the violence made her shudder.

'Well, madam, am I so disgusting that you must stare at me with that look of horror upon your face?'

Lucasta jumped.

'Oh, I – um – I beg your pardon, my lord. You look so different. . . .'

'It was a necessary disguise.'

'Oh? Why was that?'

When the viscount failed to respond to her enquiry she
looked to Mr Loughton.

'You see, Miss Symonds, the duchess wanted to draw
Miesel out, to make him think he had been seen on Hansford
Common.'

'The notice in the newspapers,' cried Lucasta. 'That was a
trap.'

'As an officer of the law I cannot be condoning traps,' said
Mr Loughton heavily. 'Her Grace assured me it was merely
a means of – ah – inducing the killer to show his hand.'

'I disguised myself as a French traveller and persuaded
Miesel that I had seen him kill Sir Talbot,' said Lord
Kennington, pouring himself a second glass of wine. 'Told
him I would take the emeralds in exchange for my silence.'

Lucasta stared at him.

'You never expected him to give them to you!'

He shrugged.

'Why not? It is too dangerous for him to sell them.'

'Then the men he met in the tavern,' she looked at Potts.
'He was plotting tonight's attack?'

'It would seem so,' replied the viscount. 'And not
completely unexpected. When he told me to meet him at
eight o'clock at the northern edge of Finsbury Fields I
guessed he might be planning something of the sort.'

Lucasta swallowed hard.

'And you walked into the trap? Knowing . . . knowing you
might be killed?'

'I did have support: Loughton and his men were following
me, only of necessity he had to keep his distance.'

'Yes, he was so far away he got himself lost!'

'Now, miss, that is unfair,' protested Mr Loughton. 'I was on the scene only moments after yourself.'

'And in those moments Lord Kennington might have died!'

'And you, Lucasta, might have got us both killed,' the viscount struck in. 'I wish to God you had stayed at home, woman.'

'So, too, do I,' she flashed at him, colour flaring in her cheeks. 'But since I am here I want to know what you plan to do next.'

'Loughton and I are going to Milk Street to arrest Miesel. It's my guess that he will be in his rooms – he is too clever to let those ruffians know where he lives so he will not yet know that his plan has failed.'

'Even if he did he wouldn't get away,' said Mr Loughton, 'I have one of my men watching him tonight.'

'I hope he's doing a better job than he did t'other night,' muttered Jacob.

Mr Loughton looked slightly abashed.

'Yes, well, even at Bow Street we cannot always get the right sort o' men. I admit we did slip up a bit in our observation of Mr Miesel.'

'You do no worse than those poor fools General Bradfield has set to watch Filwood House,' grinned the viscount. 'They still believe I am safely indoors. Come along, it is time we were away.'

Lucasta put down her glass.

'I am coming with you.'

'Oh, no, you are not. You are going home.'

'You cannot make me!'

He swung round to face her, his eyes hard and unyielding as granite.

'If you insist upon defying me I shall send you home tied

to your damned saddle! Potts, fetch the horses. You are taking Miss Symonds home.'

The groom coughed.

'Begging your pardon, sir, but I think I should come with you to Milk Street. Miesel could turn nasty, and I want to assure myself that nothing else in that establishment is – er – damaged. That is, that no innocent parties is hurt.'

The viscount stared at him.

'You refer to Mrs Jessop, I suppose.'

Jacob put up his stubbly chin and met his master's eyes with a steady gaze.

'Aye, sir, that would be it.'

Lucasta nodded approvingly, a tiny, triumphant smile curling her lips. She watched the viscount's gaze travelling from her own face to Jacob's stubborn countenance, then on to Mr Loughton's gently twinkling eyes.

'Very well.' The viscount's chair scraped back as he rose and snatched up his hat. 'Let us go.'

As he stormed out of the room, Lucasta heard him mutter, 'God protect me from overbearing women and love-sick fools!'

CHAPTER TWENTY-SEVEN

March winds tore at them as they rode back into London, gusting between the houses and swirling the dust in the darkened streets. When they reached the corner of Milk Street they drew rein. Mr Loughton beckoned to a muffled figure sheltering in a doorway.

'Any news, Price?'

The man touched his forelock.

'No, sir. He went to the tavern for his dinner, then back to his lodging. He's there now.'

'Very well. Look after the horses, Price. We'll go in.'

The shutters were up on the cheesemonger's window but light shone through the cracks. Potts knocked softly on the door and when he heard movement on the inside he said quietly, 'Sarah? It's me, Jacob.'

The door opened a crack and the widow looked out, clearly startled to find such a crowd on her doorstep. Mr Loughton stepped forward.

'No need to be afraid, Mistress. I'm here from Bow Street on a matter of business to see your lodger, Mr Miesel.'

'What he says is right, Sarah,' said Potts. 'Open the door, my dear.'

As the door opened Lucasta found the viscount gripping her arm. He turned her, forcing her to face him.

'When Miesel finds he is cornered he might turn vicious,' he said. 'Too many of us in one small room could be very dangerous. This time I must insist you do as I say, Lucasta. You will stay downstairs with Mrs Jessop, is that understood?'

He gripped her arms, giving her a little shake.

'Do you understand that, Lucasta? You must stay downstairs, promise me.'

His eyes bored into her and she read concern in their dark depths.

'I promise, Adam.'

'And promise me, whatever happens, even if Miesel should escape, you will not put yourself in any danger.'

'You have my word.'

He smiled, sliding his hands down her arms until he reached her gloved fingers, which he squeezed gently.

'Thank you, my dear.' He straightened, and gave Mrs Jessop his charming smile. 'Now, ladies if you would please wait here?'

Adam and Jacob followed Loughton up the stairs into the darkness of the landing. There was a strip of dim light coming from under one door. Loughton knocked and entered upon the echo. Miesel jumped up as they entered, scrabbling to throw a blanket over the little collection of items scattered over the bed. With surprising speed Loughton sprang forward and caught him.

'Not so fast, my fine fellow. Let's have a look at what we have here.'

Adam crossed the room. He heard Jacob give a low whistle behind him.

'Looks as if he's been caught red-handed.'

The dim lamplight glinted on the silver-backed brush and comb, an enamelled snuff-box nestled in the folds of a fine silk handkerchief bearing the initials "TB" clearly in one corner and, next to that, winking beside its leather pouch, an emerald necklace curled sinuously over a crease in the bedcover.

'No, no, it's not mine!' protested Miesel. 'It was here, like this, when I came back from my dinner. Someone is trying to pin the blame upon me.' He caught sight of Adam, still wearing his dark wig and unshaven beard and his eyes narrowed. 'Him!' he hissed out. 'The Frenchy. He tried to blackmail me. He put these things here!'

'No, no that won't work this time,' growled Loughton, not releasing his grip. 'Those fools you hired to attack this gentleman were a rum lot, Miesel. When they was caught they didn't take much persuading to tell us who put 'em up to it.'

Miesel stopped struggling. He glanced malevolently at Adam.

'So you did go to the magistrates. After the reward, was you?' When Adam said nothing he sighed. 'Very well. If that's the case I suppose it's all over.'

The fight went out of him. His shoulders drooped, his head hung to one side, signalling defeat.

'Well now, that's a sensible cove,' nodded Loughton, approvingly. 'We'll gather up this evidence and—'

'Watch out!'

Adam's shout was too late. In the brief instant that Loughton relaxed his guard, Miesel jumped back into the darkness behind him and picked up a pistol, which he now levelled at the three men. He waved them away from the door.

'You have only one shot,' said Loughton. 'There are three of us: you cannot kill us all.'

The man's lip curled savagely.

'Aye, but which one of you wants to die?' He scooped up the emeralds into his pocket.

'I didn't shoot Bradfield just to be foiled by a damned Frenchie!'

'So you *did* kill him,' said Mr Loughton.

'Aye. One of the horses had picked up a stone and we had to stop to remove it. Sir Talbot was cursing me for not being his groom. Hah! He had chosen to have me travel with him, yet as soon as things went against him it was all my fault!

'He was lecturing me, telling me I was worth nothing to him. Not a word for my loyalty over all these years, always looking to his comfort, forgoing wages when the dibs wasn't in tune.' Miesel's thin lip curled. 'It was too much, I would not listen to such ramblings any more. I pulled the carriage pistol from its holster and fired. That shook him – not so useless after all, am I? And it seemed a shame to leave the gewgaws there in the dressing case, waiting for any magpie to thieve them, so I took 'em, as recompense for all those times he couldn't pay me. Stand back!'

The words shot out as Adam moved. Immediately, the pistol was pointing at his stomach.

Adam lifted his hands and stepped back. At the same time Loughton launched himself at Miesel, knocking his hand. The pistol went off but the ball buried itself harmlessly in the plaster. Snarling, Miesel brought the butt down heavily upon Loughton's head. The Runner fell back against Jacob, both of them cannoning into Adam and in the confines of the small room it took a moment for them to untangle themselves, a moment that allowed Miesel to hurl himself out of the door.

Sarah Jessop looked enquiringly at Lucasta as they moved into the lamp-lit shop. Behind the shuttered glass the windows were full of round cheeses, piled high ready for the morning.

'You have been busy,' remarked Lucasta, looking about her.

'The morning is always the busiest time,' replied Sarah. 'I like to have the truckles ready to cut. Will you tell me what is going on? Is Jacob in trouble?'

'No, no, it is your lodger who is the villain of the piece, Mrs Jessop. They have come to arrest him.'

'Mercy me! Then I think I have a right to know the story.'

Lucasta was listening to the clump of footsteps overhead, the murmur of voices.

'It would take too long. Jacob shall tell you everything tomorrow.'

There was a change in the murmurs from the room above, one of the voices became more strident. Lucasta's mouth was dry, it was difficult to listen when the blood was pounding so heavily in her ears. There was a thud, a scuffle and a shot. Sarah gasped. The viscount's voice came from above.

'He's getting away!'

The two women stared at each other, wide-eyed, as they heard the clatter of boots on the stairs. Only for a second did they hesitate: as one, they moved towards the cheeses piled nearest the door and pushed. The pile tottered and tumbled out of the open door, thudding and rolling across the bottom of the stairs just as Miesel hurtled down. There was no room for his feet between the heavy, muslin-wrapped truckles and he fell, sprawling, into the chaos.

191

A steadier footstep sounded and Mr Loughton appeared on the bottom step, grinning broadly at the devastation.

'Oh, well done, Mistress. The villain brought down with a cheese, by Gad!'

CHAPTER TWENTY-EIGHT

Lucasta ran to the door with Mistress Jessop. She peered over the Runner's shoulder and up into the darkness.

'There was a shot—'

'Bless you, miss, no one's hurt, the bullet went harmlessly into the wall – it's a very *small* hole, Mistress,' he added quickly with a guilty glance at Sarah.

He stepped carefully between the cheeses and gripped Miesel's collar.

'Well, now, sir, I think we'll have that necklace out o' your pocket and put it in mine for safe keeping. Then it's off to the magistrates' court with you.'

'Aye, take him away,' muttered Sarah, bending to pick up one of the truckles and put it back in the window. 'Heaven knows if any of these will be of use, now.'

'Well, Mistress, there is a reward for the apprehension of this villain, and for the safe return of the Bradfield emeralds, so that might be some recompense for your troubles, eh?'

Sarah grinned.

'Aye, that it might.'

'Mistress Jessop, a thousand apologies for this upset.' Lord Kennington came down the stairs with Potts close behind him .You have taken no injury, I trust?'

'None, thank you, sir. Nothing that a little effort cannot mend.'

Potts followed his master into the shop.

'With your permission, my lord, I would like to stay here. After this kick up Mistress Jessop might be glad of a hand putting everything to rights.'

'I am sure Lord Kennington would be glad for you to remain here,' put in Lucasta. 'I know for my own part I should find it a comfort to have a good man such as yourself around the house.'

Jacob threw out his chest at this fulsome praise and Sarah's rosy cheeks grew even pinker.

'I would be glad of Mr Potts's company, miss, to be sure. If he can be spared.'

'Then it is settled,' agreed the viscount. 'I shall take your horse back to the stables, Jacob, and shall look for you at Filwood House in the morning.' He put out his hand. 'Miss Symonds, I think now it is time to take you home.'

Escorted by Lord Kennington, Lucasta followed Mr Loughton and his prisoner back to the corner of Milk Street where Price was anxiously awaiting them. He looked relieved to hand back responsibility for the horses, confiding to the viscount that he didn't understand these nervy, high-strung beasts and was much more at home looking after hardened criminals.

'If that's the case, me lad, you can keep hold o' this one,' retorted Mr Loughton, pushing Miesel forward. 'He's a thief and a murderer.' He then turned to the viscount, touching his hat. 'So I'll say goodnight to you, my lord. I shall take leave to call at Filwood House tomorrow to report how matters stand to her grace, and to take a signed deposition from you, my lord – and I shall be wanting one from you, too, miss.'

'We would not want you traipsing all over London tomorrow, Loughton, so I shall send the carriage for Miss Symonds to bring her to Filwood House, then you can talk to us all together. Shall we say at three o'clock?'

With the arrangements agreed it was time to depart. The viscount threw Lucasta into the saddle and they set off through the darkened streets, Jacob's horse trotting along beside them.

'I may soon be obliged to find myself a new groom,' remarked the viscount with a chuckle. 'I never thought Potts would become leg-shackled, but he is well and truly smitten, is he not? I wonder if he really wishes to sell cheese? If not, I must find a house on one of my estates for Jacob and his wife. What say you, Luke?' He turned his head to look at her. 'You are very quiet: are you tired, Lucasta?'

'Yes I am, desperately so.' It was an effort even to speak, but she turned her head to give him a weary smile. 'It has come upon me very suddenly. Yet it cannot be so very late.'

'It was nearing eleven when we left Milk Street.'

'It is early then, and we could go on to attend several parties, if we so wished!'

He laughed.

'I want only to wash, shave and sleep – and of those I think sleep will take precedence.'

'And you may sleep easily now, Adam, for your innocence is proven. You have done it.'

'*We* have done it.' He reached out his hand to her. 'I am truly grateful to you, Lucasta, even if fears for your safety have made me less than gracious at times.'

He squeezed her fingers. Lucasta felt a sudden constriction in her throat. She was unable to speak.

'You are free from all suspicion,' she managed at last. 'That is all that matters.'

As they rode westward the streets grew wider and their way was illuminated by streetlamps and the torchères burning outside the grander houses. When they turned into Sophia Street Lucasta was surprised to see all the windows of her mother's house ablaze with light.

'Mama has visitors. How strange, that these parties are going on: I feel I have been in a different world.' She glanced at her companion and said, shyly, 'Will you come in, my lord?'

'I think my ragged appearance would be too shocking for a drawing-room. But pray tell them the good news. After we have talked to Loughton tomorrow and matters are settled I am sure the word will spread very quickly. I hope then Lady Symonds will feel able to receive me without embarrassment.'

'There should never have been any embarrassment,' she muttered fiercely.

He smiled at her.

'You have always been my champion, Lucasta, have you not? Now, here is your estimable butler holding open the door for you. You must go in, my dear. Shall I assist you?'

'No, pray do not get down.' She slid easily from the saddle. 'My regards to Madam Duchess, my lord. I look forward to seeing her tomorrow.'

She watched him ride away before hurrying up the stairs into the house. Lady Symonds was entertaining, she was informed. A small party, in the drawing-room: perhaps Miss Symonds would care to change her muddy habit before going in? Lucasta barely heard the butler's words. Her tiredness was gone now and she was eager to share her news with her family. She almost ran to the drawing-room and burst in, unable to prevent a beaming smile breaking out upon her face.

'He is free!' she declared as she walked into the room. 'The real killer has been found, and confessed, and Adam is free!'

Silence met her words. She looked at the little group before her. It was indeed a small party. Lady Symonds was seated upon a sofa on one side of the fireplace with Camilla beside her, while Sir Hilary Collingham occupied a chair opposite. He had risen to his feet upon her entrance, and now he was the first to react to her announcement.

'A good evening to you, Miss Symonds. So Kennington's innocence is proved! Capital news! You had it from the duchess, I suppose? Lady Symonds explained to me that you was dining at Filwood House.'

'Y-yes.' As he bowed over her hand her brain raced to put together her story. Only now did she realize how impossible it would be to explain her evening's adventures. 'Yes, she was informed tonight that the real villain has been apprehended.'

'Well, thank heaven for that,' declared Lady Symonds. 'I shall send a note to the duchess tomorrow, offering my congratulations. And one to the viscount: I shall invite him to join us for dinner one day soon. Of course, we never doubted Kennington's innocence for a moment.'

'Camilla.' Lucasta bent a searching look upon her sister. 'Are you not pleased to know Lord Kennington is no longer under suspicion?'

'Of course I am.' She began to fan herself vigorously. 'It has been such a worry.'

'As indeed it would be,' nodded Sir Hilary. 'I understand you knew the viscount before coming to Town, is that not so?'

'Why yes,' replied Lady Symonds, all smiles. 'He was a

197

frequent visitor to Oaklands as a boy. Quite a favourite with us.'

'He is a fine fellow,' agreed Sir Hilary. 'But who is the real villain? How was he taken up? I am intrigued to learn more—'

With a look of pure alarm, Lady Symonds broke in quickly.

'Lucasta has been out riding all day, I doubt she has anything to add that is not mere speculation. We must wait a little for the true facts to emerge.'

Lucasta was not sure how much her mama had guessed of her activities that evening, but she took the hint and immediately disclaimed any more knowledge of the matter.

'I am sorry. I should not have burst in upon you in all my mud. Please, excuse me!'

And with this strangled apology, she fled to the seclusion of her bedchamber.

The clock was striking three the following afternoon as Lucasta was shown into the morning-room at Filwood House. She was a little disconcerted to find only Lord Kennington there to receive her.

'My godmother is in the library with Mr Loughton. He is making his report to her there.' He kissed her hand and her fingers trembled. 'You are shivering: come and sit by the fire. I hope you found your Mama and sister well when you went home last night?'

'Yes, thank you, my lord. They are delighted to know that you are no longer suspected of murder.' She hesitated. 'They assume I spent the afternoon riding with the duchess, and then dining here. I have not told them otherwise: after a little reflection I decided it would be best not to divulge my part in last night's . . . activities.'

'No,' he grinned. 'If your mama knew we had been adventuring together again, she might think me obliged to marry you. A ridiculous thought, is it not?'

She forced herself to laugh but it sounded hollow to her own ears.

'Q-quite ridiculous.'

'You have been out walking this morning.'

She looked up quickly.

'Why, yes, how do you know that?' she put her hands up to her cheeks. 'I suppose my skin is a little brown. Oh dear. I did not take a parasol with me, for although it is such a sunny day I thought it would not matter, being so early in the year. I – um – I needed some ribbons for my gown.'

A lame excuse, she thought, but she could not tell him the truth, that she did not want to listen to her mother's remarks upon betrothals and marriage settlements, nor Camilla's discussions of bridal gowns and trousseaus.

'Indeed,' she said brightly, 'the shops were so inviting that I spent much longer in Bond Street than I had planned and returned home with barely enough time to change into my dress to come here.'

It had suited her very well to be in and out of the house without a word to her family: no time for talk of weddings and betrothals to upset her.

'I see. Then you will not know. I called at Sophia Street this morning and I—'

He broke off as the door opened. Mr Giggs peeped in.

'Oh, do I intrude?' He came forward, not waiting for a reply. 'It is Miss Symonds, is it not? How do you do? You are here to see her grace, I have no doubt. She is closeted with Mr Loughton at the moment – discussing this shocking business of the murder. You know all about it, of course?'

'Yes, I—'

'I must tell you I was never more relieved than when I

heard it was all over, that the real culprit had been discovered and our dear Lord Kennington is free!'

The viscount put up a hand

'I think there are a few formalities to be gone through yet,
Mr Giggs.'

'But that is all they will be, formalities. Then we may all
be comfortable again.' He turned his smiling face back to
Lucasta. She was a little surprised. He seemed so much
more animated than when they had met at Coombe Chase.
'And you are here to see the duchess. Her grace's carriage
brought you to the door, in fact, so she must want to see you!'
He gave a little titter. 'I think she has taken quite a fancy to
you, Miss Symonds. And what a treat is in store for you, for
the duke himself is in residence! Yes, the duke, her son! I can
see by your look that you are surprised. He arrived only last
night, quite unannounced.'

'And I have not yet had time to inform Miss Symonds,' put
in the viscount through gritted teeth. Mr Giggs continued
unabashed.

'I am sure he will be delighted to meet you, my dear. He is
always eager to know her grace's little interests.'

Lucasta was not at all sure that she liked being called a
'little interest' but at that moment the door opened and the
duchess herself entered. She merely nodded to Mr Giggs but
greeted Lucasta warmly, and told her that Mr Loughton was
waiting to talk to her in the library. Giggs looked up.

'Oh? So our investigator wishes to see Miss Symonds, too?
Dear me, I had no idea you were involved in this sordid little
mystery.'

'She is not,' returned the duchess calmly. 'But since we
move in the same circles she has some knowledge of Sir
Talbot and his valet. Run along, my dear, and when you have
done you may bring Mr Loughton back here with you for a

little refreshment.'

A short time later Lucasta was on her way back to the morning-room. Her interview with Mr Loughton had not been as bad as she had feared; he had treated her with a respectful kindness, made his notes quickly and then informed her that she had nothing more to worry about.

'And Lord Kennington is completely free now?' She looked up anxiously into his craggy face.

'Well, there will be documents to be written, and a court appearance or two, but nothing to worry about. The case against Miesel is all right and tight.'

'And – and that poor boy, the one they thought was Mr Smith?'

'Oh he has been released and sent home. His mysterious benefactor stood bail for him, paid his fees and set up a fund for him and his mother. Of course, it is not for me to speculate, but I think we might guess who the benefactor might be.' He chuckled and tapped his nose. 'A generous and kind-hearted lady, wouldn't you say, miss? A great lady, indeed, she is, and one that isn't above entertaining the likes o' me to a glass o' wine.'

He was still chuckling as the footman opened the door to the morning-room and announced them.

Mr Giggs was standing before the fireplace holding forth upon some obscure subject; the viscount stood at the window, ignoring him, and the duchess was sitting on one of the satin-covered sofas, looking bored. She looked around as the door opened and beckoned to Lucasta.

'Ah, there you are. I have had the tea tray sent up, you see, and wine for those who prefer it. Do pray come and sit by me, my child. Mr Giggs, I fear we are keeping you from your studies. Pray, do not feel you are obliged to entertain us any longer.'

'No, no, ma'am, I have nothing urgent to attend to, I promise you. I made sure all was in order before I came downstairs today: I believe his grace means to join us, and I would not be thought backward in any attention.'

'Oh, I am sure no one could think you backward, sir,' murmured the viscount. He poured a glass of wine and handed it to Mr Loughton.

'I think we owe you our thanks, sir.'

'I was doing no more than my job, my lord,' came the modest reply. 'Although some of your lordship's plans was perhaps a little unconventional, but we shall say no more o' that.' He cast a quick glance at Mr Giggs, whose attention at that moment was given to accepting a cup of tea from the duchess.

Lucasta felt sure that Giggs would have questioned Mr Loughton further about the viscount's unconventional plans if the entrance of the Duke of Filwood had not caused a timely diversion. She observed the duke with interest. He was dressed in some magnificence in a green velvet frock-coat with matching knee breeches and a white embroidered waistcoat. Upon his head was a powdered wig and in the froth of lace at his throat a diamond winked when he moved. He had inherited his mother's height and handsome looks but none of her charm: there was no humour in his blue eyes and no ready smile hovering about his thin lips. He was, she thought, very much aware of his elevated status.

It was clear to Lucasta that the duke viewed his mother's involvement in Sir Talbot's murder with abhorrence. Mr Giggs was quick to explain to him the reason for Mr Loughton's presence.

'So you see, Your Grace, Lord Kennington has been cleared. The dark shadow of suspicion no longer hangs over this family.'

The duke's brows rose.

'There never was a shadow of suspicion over this family, Mr Giggs. There is no blood line between the Filwoods and the Kenningtons. Nevertheless, I am glad the matter is now resolved, Adam.'

The viscount inclined his head.

'Thank you, Charles. That is very gracious of you.'

'Yes, I am relieved that the whole matter is now concluded,' he announced, when Mr Loughton had taken his leave. 'Although perhaps I should congratulate you, Mama, upon your choice of operative: that fellow does appear to have been very thorough.'

'Oh he is very good, I am sure,' agreed Mr Giggs with another titter. 'But he is not quite as clever as all that.' He looked about him to make sure that he had everyone's attention before continuing. 'He was supposed to talk to anyone who might have some information, but there is one person he missed. Someone who might have thrown a little light on this case much earlier. Myself.'

'And just what do you know about anything?' asked the viscount scornfully.

Giggs smirked.

'I would tell you, my lord, only – perhaps it should be some other time.' His eyes flickered towards Lucasta. 'We have a guest, you know.'

'Miss Symonds has been party to a great many confidences since this affair blew up,' the duchess responded with a reassuring look towards Lucasta. 'I think we may trust her.'

'There you are,' nodded the viscount. 'My godmother vouches for Miss Symonds so you may safely divulge your secrets, Giggs. Tell us what you know, although I'll wager it is nothing of significance.'

Mr Giggs drew himself up at this, and cast the viscount a look of dislike.

'Oh, I think you will find it is of significance, Lord Kennington. I grant you, my lord that I was not party to the events upon Hansford Common, but I do know something of the mysterious Mr Smith.'

Lucasta froze. The fingers holding her teacup shook slightly but she dared not put the cup back in its saucer, fearing the clatter would draw attention to herself.

Lord Kennington was looking intently at Giggs. He said carefully, 'Loughton informed us that Mr Smith is no longer a suspect in this case.'

'Perhaps not, but he is still of interest to those of us gathered here. You, my lord, because you took the young man up in the first place, and were responsible for introducing him into her grace's household—'

'Damnation man,' exclaimed the viscount, 'be done with your long periods and tell us what you think you know!'

'Yes, Giggs,' said the duke, flicking away his coat tails and sitting down. 'If you know something, you should declare it immediately.'

'Very well, Your Grace, I will. This mysterious Mr Smith was her grace's lover!'

CHAPTER TWENTY-NINE

For a long moment Lucasta thought she had suddenly gone deaf. Mr Giggs's announcement produced a profound silence and looks of frozen amazement upon the faces of his audi- tors. Then Lucasta's senses righted themselves, she heard the steady tick, tick of the clock, and the rattle of a teacup in its saucer. It took her a little while to realize it was her own cup that had come to rest. She looked across the room at the viscount. As if aware of her gaze he met her eyes, his own brimful of wicked laughter, but she was too horrified to share it. Using both hands, she carefully put her cup and saucer on the table, afraid that at any moment she might drop them.

'Indeed, Mr Giggs?' the duchess's voice held only the slightest tremor. 'And how came you to this conclusion?'

'By the evidence of my own eyes,' he said. 'I knew this Smith for a sneaking rascal the first time I met him, for he was careful never to be alone with me, or to be in my company for more than a few moments. I know not how he prevailed upon Lord Kennington for his acquaintance, but he was a plausible rogue and no doubt he cozened the viscount thoroughly—'

'This is all nonsense!'

The duke held up his hand.

'We will hear him out, Kennington, if you please.'

Mr Giggs bowed to him.

'Thank you, Your Grace. As you are aware, I see my position in your dear mother's household as a protector and mentor, someone to guide her through the pitfalls of her widowhood.'

The duchess blinked.

'I beg your pardon?'

'Grief can affect us all in different ways, dear ma'am. I am aware of your dear son's concerns, that without the steadying influence of a husband it is only too easy for a weak female to be led astray.'

'Dear me.' The duchess drew out her handkerchief and pressed it to her lips. 'And – and you think I have been – er – led astray?'

'It was plain to me, ma'am, that as soon as this young man entered Coombe Chase he set out to ensnare you. Why, the very first time I met him he had already breached your defences. When I walked into the room you were caressing his face!'

Lucasta choked.

'And not only that,' continued Mr Giggs, warming to his theme, 'her grace was very anxious to pursue the – ah – friendship. A slight indisposition made it necessary for me to keep to my room, but I am well aware that during his brief stay at Coombe Chase the young man spent all his time with the duchess, driving around the country, even accompanying her to church!'

'Well there is nothing shameful in that,' remarked the duchess.

'But you cannot deny that when the young man took his leave you embraced him most affectionately.' Giggs turned to address the duke. 'They were in the hall at the time, you see. I had slipped out of my sickbed in search of a little wine to help me sleep and happened to be on the balcony as this affecting scene took place.'

'Just how long did this young man spend at Coombe Chase, Mama?' asked the duke.

'Two nights,' she replied. 'Hardly sufficient time for a torrid affair, Charles.'

'Ah, if only that were true,' exclaimed Mr Giggs, shaking his head.

The duchess looked at him, a frown creasing her brow.

'If you have been bribing my servants, sir—'

'No, no, nothing like that. Your staff are all far too loyal to admit any criticism of you, Your Grace. Even when I question them directly they tell me nothing.'

'I am glad to hear it,' she replied grimly. 'I pay them very well and they know I keep no disloyal servants.'

'So you are basing your allegations upon a conjecture,' put in the viscount, his lip curling. 'A couple of friendly gestures and a day's driving about the countryside. That hardly amounts to scandalous behaviour, Giggs.'

'If that were all, I would not have written to the duke and begged him to come to Town to confront his mama with this matter. But there is proof, incontrovertible proof.'

'A love-child, perhaps?' murmured the duchess.

'Mama, please.' The duke looked pained. 'Continue, Mr Giggs.'

'It grieves me to say that her grace was so taken in by this young man that she connived at his plan. She had him placed in the bedroom adjoining her own and' – he reached into his pocket – 'if you want even more proof of their dalliance, I found this upon the floor of her grace's bedchamber!'

He unfolded a small paper to reveal a lock of honey-brown hair.

'Hell and damnation,' muttered the viscount, staring at the hair, which lay upon the paper, curled into a perfect question mark.

'I see it now,' declared Mr Giggs. 'There they were, late that night, cutting off locks of hair – exchanging love tokens!'

The duke rose and took a step forward. He raised his quizzing glass to inspect the curl more closely.

'This was found upon the floor of my mother's bedchamber you say. By whom was it found?'

'By me,' Mr Gggs beamed. 'I found it upon the floor, by the dressing-table, the very day after this Mr Smith had arrived.' He was almost jumping up and down with excitement now. 'It is the exact shade of the scoundrel's hair! Well, ma'am, what have you to say to that?'

As all eyes turned to the duchess, Lucasta knew she must speak out.

'Your Grace, this is monstrous. I—'

The duchess's hand shot out and gripped her wrist.

'I know what you are going to say, Miss Symonds. You are shocked by these revelations, and so you should be, for you are a young woman, gently reared and not yet married. I, on the other hand, am a widow of many years' standing. However, I am not in my dotage. If I wish to take a lover, I think that it is entirely my business. I never played your father false when he was alive, Charles, but I do not think he would begrudge me a little excitement now, if I should wish for it.'

A heavy silence filled the room. Lucasta stared at her.

'You – you are admitting it?' she asked, her voice scarcely above a whisper.

The duchess met her eyes, her face alive with laughter.

'Why not? It quite enhances my reputation, to capture such a *young* man.'

The viscount gave a shout of laughter.

'Godmama, you are quite shameless!'

'No, in fact I have always been most discreet.' She bent her smiling eyes upon her son. 'Well, Charles?'

The duke did not appear to hear her. His eyes were fixed upon Mr Giggs.

'Do you tell me that you took it upon yourself to enter my mother's chamber, to invade her private apartments in search of evidence for your tawdry little story?'

'Your Grace, I – I was trying to establish—'

'You took it upon yourself to pry into the personal affairs of my mother – my mother, the Duchess of Filwood, in whose veins runs the blood of royalty?'

'But I thought you wanted – I was trying to preserve your good name!' Giggs clasped his hands together, cringing before the duke's wrathful figure.

'And you think that you, a snivelling little cleric, have the right to snoop, to question my mother's servants on the pretence of *preserving my good name*? Bah! You disgust me. You are to be gone from this house within the hour, do you understand?'

'Your Grace, I—'

'Enough from you, sirrah. Get out! And if one word of these allegations ever reaches my ears again I shall make sure you suffer for it!'

Muttering incoherently, Giggs scurried to the door to make a hasty and undignified exit.

'Oh, well done, Charles,' declared the duchess.

'I am aware that we have not always seen eye to eye, Mama, but I think in this instance I owe you an apology.'

'Thank you, that is very handsomely said. Perhaps now you will allow me to find a more agreeable companion to bear me company.'

'It shall be as you wish, Mama. Although I hope you do not mean to return to Coombe Chase just yet. I have it in mind to find me a wife, and would welcome your assistance.'

'Well, this is a day for surprises,' grinned the viscount.

'Thank you, Kennington, but it is no laughing matter. And it would do you no harm to be thinking of settling down.'

'Oh I am, Filwood, I am.' He smiled across the room at Lucasta. 'I have already set my plans in motion.'

Lucasta leapt to her feet.

'If you will excuse me, I think I must go home. We – um – we are to go to the play tonight, and I must prepare.'

'Yes, of course, my dear. How selfish of me to keep you here for so long.' The duchess rose. 'I shall order the carriage immediately.'

The viscount was across the room in a two strides.

'I should very much like to accompany you to Sophia Street.'

Lucasta shook her head. She could not bear the thought of watching him tell Camilla that he was now free to marry her. Not yet.

'No, thank you. You are very kind, but I would prefer to return home alone.'

Sitting in the duchess's elegant carriage, Lucasta considered her situation. She was glad she had been able to help prove Adam's innocence. At first she had thought it was all that mattered, that there would be no greater joy than knowing Camilla could marry the man of her choice, but she felt no joy now at the prospect, only a searing, aching jealousy. What did Camilla know of Adam? She had not travelled with him for miles in an open carriage, talking of everything and nothing, spent the night in a ramshackle inn, shared such adventures with him. Lucasta choked back a sob. How was she to bear it, having Adam as her brother-in-law? Papa would take great pleasure in parading Camilla's success before her, prolonging her misery. Some demon inside her head whispered that she should inform her mama of the duke's arrival and his avowed intention to find a wife. *That* would be a conquest indeed and one she was sure Camilla would wish to attempt. But no, if Adam wanted to marry Camilla she would put no more obstacles in his way; he had suffered enough. If he wanted Camilla he must have her. But would their marriage be a success? Her demon persisted. Would she be able to read his moods, to joke him out of his bad temper, or enjoy his good humour?

'She will learn,' she told herself fiercely. 'She will learn to make him happy!'

But what of her own future? What happiness was there now for her? At the moment she could see none, only a long, empty future full of loneliness. She gave herself a mental shake. This mood could not last; just because she fancied herself in love with Adam did not mean there could be no happiness in the future, it was merely that she was unable to see it. Suddenly, she wanted to go home, to Oaklands, to hide in the tree house with her books and her drawing pad and wait for this crippling pain to ease. She was sure her mama would agree to her leaving. After all, she had done nothing but fall from one scrape into another, and there was no eligible suitor in view to make it worthwhile keeping her in Town. No, her mama would be only too pleased to send her home.

*

When the carriage drew up in Sophia Street she ran into the house and made her way directly to the morning-room, silently rehearsing her excuses for leaving Town. She opened the door, words ready upon her lips, but they were not uttered, for she could only stand and stare at the scene that met her eyes.

Camilla was dancing around the room, singing while her mother was at her writing desk, surrounded by lists and notes. When she saw Lucasta in the doorway, Camilla skipped over to her.

'Oh Lucasta, is it not wonderful? He loves me and we are to be married as soon as maybe – by special licence!' Camilla kissed her. 'Oh my dear, are you not happy for me?'

Lucasta dragged up a smile.

'Very happy, for you. But how is this? When was all this arranged?'

Camilla was off again, dancing around the room.

'It was all arranged this morning, while you were in Bond Street! Oh I am the happiest of women!'

'I – I don't understand,' said Lucasta. 'Pray, Camilla, stop still long enough to tell me the whole.'

'I cannot stop, I am too excited! Adam came and explained everything, and— Oh Mama, have you finished the list yet? Is there not time to go begin shopping for my wedding clothes tonight?'

'No, of course there is not!' Lady Symonds smiled affectionately at Camilla. 'Silly child, have you forgotten we are promised to go to the play?'

'Oh, what care I for plays when there is a wedding to be arranged. Oh, Lucasta, I am marrying the most charming, most handsome man in the world!' She threw herself into her sister's arms again and Lucasta hugged her, blinking back her own tears.

'Of course you are, my dear.'

Detaching herself gently, Lucasta left Camilla to her raptures. A special licence – she should not be surprised. Adam had been forced to hide his feelings for his bride for long enough. A sob escaped her. It was too much, she could not pretend to be happy, so it would be better if she left them immediately. Thankfully, it was a new month and her pin money had so far not been touched. She would catch the night mail and go home.

CHAPTER THIRTY

The tree house was just as Lucasta remembered it, creaking and draughty. It seemed a lifetime since she had climbed the steps, not merely a few weeks. She stacked a pile of books in one corner, proof of the extensive programme of reading she had set herself for the next few months. She had been at Oaklands for a week now and there was still no word from Town. Her father had been delighted with the news of the forthcoming marriage, and had set off for London immediately, leaving Lucasta to run the house alone. There was plenty of housework to be done and with her reading, music, needlework and drawing to fill her leisure time Lucasta tried her best to blot out the memories of the past few weeks. Yet however hard she tried, there was always Adam's shadow at her side, so real that sometimes she spoke out loud to him, or turned, expecting to find him beside her, and aware of an aching disappointment when she realized he was not there.

Lucasta gazed out of the windows, taking in the vivid blue and white April sky and the drifts of yellow daffodils that surrounded the tree house. This was where she belonged, she told herself firmly. This was her home. Her father might resent her presence, but as long as she could retreat occasionally to her own special place she hoped she could be happy. She settled herself down on the floor to read. The cushions felt damp and cold to her touch but she had her thick cloak to wrap about her and they provided a softer seat than the wooden boards. She lifted a book from the pile and opened it, running her hands over the silky smooth pages. It was a novel, nothing improving at all, but it would pass the time, and perhaps even allow her to forget her unhappiness for a while. The wind played around the tree house, rattling loose windows, whistling through a crack in the frame but then over the sounds of nature she heard the tread of footsteps on the staircase. She sighed and put down her book. What had she forgotten to do? She had collected the eggs, set the scullerymaid to work clearing out the dairy and given Cook instructions for dinner. Had she remembered to tell Mrs Piggott about the sheet that needed mending?

The door creaked on its hinges and as it opened wider, she blinked in surprise.

'Squire Woodcote!'

'Aye. You weren't expecting me, now, were you Miss Symonds?'

She scrambled to her feet as the squire stepped into the room, wheezing slightly.

'N-no, indeed. Papa is not at home today.'

'Oh, I am well aware o' that. It's you I've come to see.'

'Shall we go back to the house, then? I think—'

'Oh no, this will do us very well,' he interrupted, closing the door and planting himself squarely in front of it. Even at a distance he stank of brandy. A shiver of unease ran through Lucasta. She tried to hide it beneath a smile.

'Oh, but there is nowhere to sit here. Let us go to the house and I will order refreshments—'

'I didn't come here to make polite conversation with you, madam.' He took a step towards her. 'There's some unfinished business between us.'

'I think not, sir.' She drew her cloak more closely about her as if to screen herself from the hungry look in his bloodshot eyes.

'Oh, I think so, madam. You ran out on me on our wedding day.'

'I had not agreed to any wedding.'

He swore viciously and spat on the floor.

'It was your father's decision, not yours, girl! When have I given you cause to think ill of me – haven't I always been kind to you? And what do I get for all my trouble? You run away, and leave me a laughing stock.'

'Squire Woodcote, I assure you—'

'Save your breath, missy.' He began to unbutton his riding coat. 'I've been waitin' for you to come back, promising myself that I'd have you, one way or t'other. Mebbe if you please me I won't hurt you too much.'

She took a step backwards.

'I – um – Mama told me you were looking elsewhere for a bride, sir. If that is so what can you want with me?'

'No one makes a fool o' me, Miss Symonds. I was lookin' forward to bedding you, girl, but you thought yourself too good for me, ain't that true?' He took another step towards her. 'Thought to get yourself a fine husband like Miss Camilla, no doubt. But when I've finished with you, no decent man will want you!'

'No!'

As he lunged at her, Lucasta sidestepped and ran for the door but he was too quick. One hand fastened on her cloak, ripping it from her shoulders and the other grabbed her arm, yanking her cruelly back towards him.

'Not so fast, my dear: you are not leaving here until I have finished with you.'

'Let me go!'

She struggled in his arms, trying to beat him with her fists but he merely laughed and wrestled her to the floor, toppling the pile of books. Lucasta found herself pinned down on the cushions. Woodcote's hands ripped at her gown, tearing away the muslin around her neck. With a growl he leaned down to kiss her and she turned her face away, gagging at the smell of tobacco and brandy and onions mixed in his hot breath. With all her strength Lucasta struck out, raking her fingernails down his cheek. Woodcote let out a curse and dealt her a heavy blow. Her head snapped back; everything went black. She tasted blood in her mouth and as her vision cleared she found Woodcote kneeling across her, pinning her with his weight while his hands scrabbled to unbutton his breeches.

'Now, Miss Lucasta Symonds, now we shall see!'

He was leering down at her; pulling up her skirts.

'No,' she groaned, pushing at him.

He swatted her hands away. She knew she needed to concentrate if she was to fight him, but it was so hard, so much effort to resist him and she was tiring. She uttered up a desperate prayer. The door creaked on its hinges and Lucasta peered around the squire's body in time to see Lord Kennington step into the room. It could not be true. How could it be Adam? She had prayed for someone to save her but surely she had conjured him up, a wishful dream. But he could not be a dream, for he was carrying a basket and surely if he was the saviour of her dreams he would be carrying a sword, not a basket.

'Adam!' she tried to cry out, but she was not sure if she had made any sound.

The viscount put down the basket and advanced upon the squire, who was not yet aware of his presence. The next moment the leaden weight had been lifted from her. With a cry of rage the squire twisted to face his opponent and was met with a crashing blow to the jaw. He crumpled, unconscious, and Adam turned from him to kneel beside Lucasta.

'Thank God I was in time. Are you all right?'

She reached out and he took her fingers in a firm, comforting clasp.

'You are safe now, Lucasta.' He smiled down at her. 'Now we are equal, for this time I have rescued *you*.'

With his free hand he straightened her petticoats, smoothing them down as if it was the most natural thing in the world for him to do. A groan and a string of curses announced that Squire Woodcote had regained consciousness. Adam pressed her hand and gave her another reassuring smile.

'Excuse me for a moment: I have unfinished business.'

He swung away from her and grabbed the back of the squire's collar.

'I think you have outworn your welcome here, sir.'

Ignoring the squire's protests he pushed him out through the door and Lucasta heard the clatter and bump of a body falling down the steps. Alone in the tree house, she heard the sound of further grunts and thuds and she tried hard not to imagine what was going on at the base of the old lime. She struggled to sit up and was rearranging the muslin fichu around her neck when Adam returned.

'He is gone. You need not worry now, Lucasta, he will not trouble you again.'

'Thank you.'

He bent a searching gaze upon her.

'And you are not hurt?'

'N-no,' she felt her lip. The split was inside her mouth and had already stopped bleeding. 'A few bruises, nothing more.'

'Thank heaven for that.'

Now that the danger was over she could think clearly again. The familiar pain returned, replacing her recent fear. It was too cruel, she was not ready to meet Adam again yet. Just seeing him was like a knife slicing into her heart.

'What – what are you doing here?' The words came out as a croak.

'I came to find you.'

He crossed the room and picked up the wicker basket. Heavens! Please do not say Camilla had planned a lover's picnic in the tree-house.

'I have brought you a present.' He reached into the basket and pulled out a squirming bundle of fur and legs.

'Oh – oh, thank you!' She reached out to take the puppy. The little dog struggled for a moment, one white ear flapping wildly but as Lucasta held her close she stopped and nuzzled her chin. 'It is the puppy from Coombe Chase! Thank you so much: I shall call her Nutmeg.'

Adam smiled.

'She remembers you,' he said, sitting down beside her. 'Godmama asked me to bring her to you.'

'Oh that is kind of Madam Duchess. She will be company for me.' She fondled the puppy, aware that Adam was watching her.

'Why did you run away?'

She could not meet his eyes. Perhaps she should try standing up. Gently she put the puppy back in the basket.

'I didn't run away. I – um – I was homesick.' She felt his hand under her elbow as she got to her feet.

'Was there nothing in Town worth staying for?'

She turned away to gaze out of the window, blinking away hot tears.

'No.'

'Godmama was most put out.'

She squeezed her eyes shut and struggled to speak to him.

'I am sorry. I did write to her. . . .'

'Yes. Some tarradiddle about not wanting to be a burden.' He paused. 'You have not asked me yet about the wedding.'

Another twist of the knife.

'Oh, yes. How – how was it?'

'Oh, a very elegant affair. The bride was beautiful, of course; the bride's mama cried throughout most of the proceedings but Sir Hilary bore up manfully.'

'Sir Hilary! Was he there, then?'

She looked up to find him standing far too close, that disturbing twinkle in his grey eyes.

'Of course – who else should be there?'

'I don't know,' she replied hastily, flustered by his near-ness. 'I – I never thought of him as your particular friend, but I suppose you must have a groomsman – I cannot see what I have said that is so funny,' she ended crossly.

'No, you wouldn't,' he chuckled, drawing her into his arms. 'But you see, my sweet goose-cap, Sir Hilary was the *groom*.'

She was putting out her hands to hold him off when the significance of his words reached her brain. She stopped and stared up at him.

'Camilla married *Sir Hilary*? But – but that's impossible! She was engaged to you!'

'Never officially. If you had not flounced out of the house—'

'I did not flounce out of the house!'

'If you had not left in such a hurry you would have known all this a week ago. The morning after Miesel was arrested I called at Sophia Street. You were out, shopping if I recall. It was clear to me that Camilla had had a change of heart and no longer wished to marry me, so we decided that it would be foolish to go ahead with the betrothal. Since very few people knew the secret we thought it would be safe to put it behind us. I understand Sir Hilary called shortly after that, proposed and was accepted.'

She stared up at him, her eyes filling with tears.

'Oh heartless, *heartless* Camilla, to treat you thus after all you had been through!'

'No, no she treated me very well. It is many weeks since I thought myself in love with her.'

But Lucasta was not listening.

'Oh Adam I am so sorry, I would not have you unhappy for the world.'

'I am *not* unhappy. Lucasta—'

She gripped his jacket, looking up at him.

'You must forget her.'

'I have forgotten her,' he said promptly.

'Ah no, you are pretending, hiding your broken heart—'

She got no further. The viscount, realizing that she was not listening to anything he said, decided to take more drastic action. He cupped her chin with his hand, tilted up her face and kissed her.

The shock of his mouth upon hers caused Lucasta's lips to part and she found herself being kissed so ruthlessly, so expertly, that her senses reeled. Hot, giddy sensations poured through her body. She felt quite unsteady and was obliged to slide her arms around Adam's neck for support. His own arms tightened around her, hugging her to him until she was aware of her body melting into his, even pressing against him. At last he lifted his head but he did not release his hold of her and she rested her cheek against his chest, sighing deeply.

'Oh,' she murmured into his waistcoat. 'Did you say you were *not* married?'

'Not yet. You only have to say the word and that can be remedied almost at once. Here, if you like. However, I would very much like to take you back to Town: Godmama tells me she wishes to dance at our wedding.'

She raised her head, smiled at him lovingly.

'Then we will go back. I cannot deny Madam Duchess anything, especially when she has given me such a sweet little puppy.'

He kissed her again.

'Good. Then we shall set out tomorrow, and be married at Filwood House by special licence.'

She looked down at the expectant, furry little face staring up at her from the basket.

'What about Nutmeg?'

'I beg your pardon?'

'Nutmeg – my puppy.'

'Leave her here until we return from our honeymoon.'

'We cannot leave her behind – she has only just left her mother; we cannot abandon her as well.'

'We are not abandoning her. Well, we are, but only for a short time.'

Lucasta shook her head.

'No, we must take her to London.'

'And what happens to her while we are on our honeymoon?'

Lucasta paused, then looked up shyly.

'Could we not take her with us?'

'I am not taking a dog on honeymoon!'

'Oh. Is it not permitted?'

'Most definitely not.'

She peeped up at him through her lashes, her eyes coming

to rest upon his mouth, set now in a determined line. It quirked at one corner and she twinkled up at him.

'Are you sure?'

'Most sure,' he said, bringing his mouth down to capture hers once more. She responded immediately, matching his desire with her own, equally urgent longing. He held her against him, breathing raggedly into her hair.

'You are a minx,' he muttered, nibbling her ear. 'But my plans for our honeymoon do not involve looking after a dog.'

She shivered delightfully in his arms.

'Very well,' she said meekly. 'Perhaps we could take her back to Coombe Chase: she could stay with her mother until we return. Is it going to be a long honeymoon?'

She looked up as she spoke, the breath catching in her throat as she saw the look in his eyes. His arms tightened around her.

'Yes, my love,' he said, lowering his head once more. 'I think it might last a lifetime.'